THE

BLIND BROTHER:

A Story of
THE PENNSYLVANIA
COAL MINES

BY
HOMER GREENE

THE BLIND BROTHER.
CHAPTER I.
LOST IN THE MINE.

The Dryden Mine, in the Susquehanna coal-fields of Pennsylvania, was worked out and abandoned long ago. To-day its headings and airways and chambers echo only to the occasional fall of loosened slate, or to the drip of water from the roof. Its pillars, robbed by retreating workmen, are crumbling and rusty, and those of its props which are still standing have become mouldy and rotten. The rats that once scampered through its galleries deserted it along with human kind, and its very name, from long disuse, has acquired an unaccustomed sound.

But twenty years ago there was no[12] busier mine than the Dryden from Carbondale to Nanticoke. Two hundred and thirty men and boys went by the slope into it every morning, and came out from it every night. They were simple and unlearned, these men and boys, rugged and rude, rough and reckless at times, but manly, heroic, and kindhearted.

Up in the Lackawanna region a strike had been in progress for nearly two weeks. Efforts had been made by the strikers to persuade the miners down the valley to join them, but at first without success.

Then a committee of one hundred came down to appeal and to intimidate. In squads of ten or more they visited the mines in the region, and, in the course of their journeyings, had come to the Dryden Slope. They had induced the miners to go out at all the workings they had thus far entered, and were no less successful here. It required persuasion, sometimes threats, sometimes, indeed, even blows, for the miners in Dryden Slope had no cause of complaint against their employers; they earned good wages, and were content.

[13]

But, twenty years ago, miners who kept at work against the wishes of their fellows while a strike was in progress, were called "black-legs," were treated with contempt, waylaid and beaten, and sometimes killed.

So the men in the Dryden Mine yielded; and soon, down the chambers and along the headings, toward the foot of the slope, came little groups, with dinner-pails and tools, discussing earnestly, often bitterly, the situation and the prospect.

The members of a party of fifteen or twenty, that came down the airway from the tier of chambers on the new north heading, were holding an especially animated conversation. Fully one-half of the men were visiting strikers. They were all walking, in single file, along the route by which the mine-cars went.

For some distance from the new chambers the car-track was laid in the airway; then it turned down through an entrance into the heading, and from that point followed the heading to the foot of the slope. Where the route crossed from the airway to the heading, the space between the[14] pillars had been carefully boarded across, so that the air current should not be turned aside; and a door had been placed in the boarding, to be opened whenever the cars approached, and shut as soon as they had passed by.

That door was attended by a boy.

To this point the party had now come, and one by one filed through the opening, while Bennie, the door-boy, stood holding back the door to let them pass.

"Ho, Jack, tak' the door-boy wi' ye!" shouted some one in the rear.

The great, broad-shouldered, rough-bearded man who led the procession turned back to where Bennie, apparently lost in astonishment at this unusual occurrence, still stood, with his hand on the door.

"Come along, lad!" he said; "come along! Ye'll have a gret play-spell noo."

"I can't leave the door, sir," answered Bennie. "The cars'll be comin' soon."

"Ye need na min' the cars. Come along wi' ye, I say!"

"But I can't go till Tom comes, anyway, you know."

[15]

The man came a step closer. He had the frame of a giant. The others who passed by were like children beside him. Then one of the men who worked in the mine, and who knew Bennie, came through the doorway, the last in the group, and said,—

"Don't hurt the boy; let him alone. His brother'll take him out; he always does."

All this time Bennie stood quite still, with his hand on the door, never turning his head.

It was a strange thing for a boy to stand motionless like that, and look neither to the right nor the left, while an excited group of men passed by, one of whom had stopped and approached him, as if he meant him harm. It roused the curiosity of "Jack the Giant," as the miners called him, and, plucking his lamp from his cap, he flashed the light of it up into Bennie's face.

The boy did not stir; no muscle of his face moved; even his eyes remained open and fixed.

[16]

"Why, lad! lad! What's the matter wi' ye?" There was tenderness in the giant's voice as he spoke, and tenderness in his bearded face as Bennie answered,—

"Don't you know? I'm blind."

"Blind! An' a-workin' i' the mines?"

"Oh, a body don't have to see to 'tend door, you know. All I've to do is to open it when I hear the cars a-comin', an' to shut it when they get by."

"Aye, that's true; but ye did na get here alone. Who helpit ye?"

Bennie's face lighted up with pleasure, as he answered,—

"Oh, that's Tom! He helps me. I couldn't get along without him; I couldn't do *any thing* without Tom."

The man's interest and compassion had grown, as the conversation lengthened, and he was charmed by the voice of the child. It had in it that touch of pathos that often lingers in the voices of the blind. He would hear more of it.

"Sit ye, lad," he said; "sit ye, an' tell me aboot Tom, an' aboot yoursel', an' a' ye can remember."

[17]

Then they sat down on the rude bench together, with the roughly hewn pillar of coal at their backs, blind Bennie and Jack Rennie, the giant, and while one told the story of his blindness, and his blessings, and his hopes, the other listened with tender earnestness, almost with tears.

Bennie told first about Tom, his brother, who was fourteen years old, two years older than himself. Tom was so good to him; and Tom could see, could see as well as anybody. "Why," he exclaimed, "Tom can see *every thing!*"

Then he told about his blindness; how he had been blind ever since he could remember. But there was a doctor, he said, who came up once from Philadelphia to visit Major Dryden, before the major died; and he had chanced to see Tom and Bennie up by the mines, and had looked at Bennie's eyes, and said he thought, if the boy could go to Philadelphia and have treatment, that sight might be restored.

Tom asked how much it would cost, and the doctor said, "Oh, maybe a hundred dollars;" and then some one came and[18] called the doctor away, and they had never seen him since.

But Tom resolved that Bennie should go to Philadelphia, if ever he could save money enough to send him.

Tom was a driver-boy in Dryden Slope, and his meagre earnings went mostly to buy food and clothing for the little family. But the dollar or two that he had been accustomed to spend each month for himself he began now to lay aside for Bennie.

Bennie knew about it, of course, and rejoiced greatly at the prospect in store for him, but expressed much discontent because he, himself, could not help to obtain the fund which was to cure him. Then Tom, with the aid of the kindhearted mine superintendent, found employment for his brother as a door-boy in Dryden Slope, and Bennie was happy. It wasn't absolutely necessary that a door-boy should see; if he had good hearing he could get along very well.

So every morning Bennie went down the slope with Tom, and climbed into an empty mine-car, and Tom's mule drew them, rattling[19] along the heading, till they reached, almost a mile from the foot of the slope, the doorway where Bennie staid.

2

Then Tom went on, with the empty cars, up to the new tier of chambers, and brought the loaded cars back. Every day he passed through Bennie's doorway on three round trips in the forenoon, and three round trips in the afternoon; and every day, when the noon-hour came, he stopped on the down-trip, and sat with Bennie on the bench by the door, and both ate from one pail the dinner prepared for them by their mother.

When quitting time came, and Tom went down to the foot of the slope with his last trip for the day, Bennie climbed to the top of a load, and rode out, or else, with his hands on the last car of the trip, walked safely along behind.

"And Tom and me together have a'most twenty dollars saved now!" said the boy exultingly. "An' we've only got to get eighty dollars more, an' then I can go an' buy back the sight into my eyes; an' then Tom an' me we're goin' to work together all our lives. Tom, he's goin' to get a[20] chamber an' be a miner, an' I'm goin' to be Tom's laborer till I learn how to mine, an' then we're goin' to take a contract together, an' hire laborers, an' get rich, an' then—why, then Mommie won't have to work any more!"

It was like a glimpse of a better world to hear this boy talk. The most favored child of wealth that ever revelled seeing in the sunlight has had no hope, no courage, no sublimity of faith, that could compare with those of this blind son of poverty and toil. He had his high ambition, and that was to work. He had his sweet hope to be fulfilled, and that was to see. He had his earthly shrine, and that was where his mother sat. And he had his hero of heroes, and that was Tom.

There was no quality of human goodness, or bravery, or excellence of any kind, that he did not ascribe to Tom. He would sooner have disbelieved all of his four remaining senses than have believed that Tom would say an unkind word to Mommie or to him, or be guilty of a mean act towards any one.

[21]

Bennie's faith in Tom was fully justified. No nineteenth century boy could have been more manly, no knight of old could have been more true and tender, than was Tom to the two beings whom he loved best upon all the earth.

"But the father, laddie," said Jack, still charmed and curious; "whaur's the father?"

"Dead," answered Bennie. "He came from the old country first, an' then he sent for Mommie an' us, an' w'en we got here he was dead."

"Ah, but that was awfu' sad for the mither! Took wi' the fever, was he?"

"No; killed in the mine. Top coal fell an' struck him. That's the way they found him. We didn't see him, you know. That was two weeks before me an' Tom an' Mommie got here. I wasn't but four years old then, but I can remember how Mommie cried. She didn't have much time to cry, though, 'cause she had to work so hard. Mommie's al'ays had to work so hard," added Bennie, reflectively.

The man began to move, nervously, on[22] the bench. It was apparent that some strong emotion was taking hold of him. He lifted the lamp from his cap again and held it up close to Bennie's face.

"Killed, said ye—i' the mine—top coal fell?"

"Yes, an' struck him on the head; they said he didn't ever know what killed him."

The brawny hand trembled so that the flame from the spout of the little lamp went up in tiny waves.

"Whaur—whaur happenit it—i' what place—i' what mine?"

"Up in Carbondale. No. 6 shaft, I think it was; yes, No. 6."

Bennie spoke somewhat hesitatingly. His quick ear had caught the change in the man's voice, and he did not know what it could mean.

"His name, lad! gi' me the father's name!"

The giant's huge hand dropped upon Bennie's little one, and held it in a painful grasp. The boy started to his feet in fear.

"You won't hurt me, sir! Please don't hurt me; I can't see!"

[23]

"Not for the warld, lad; not for the whole warld. But I must ha' the father's name; tell me the father's name, quick!"

"Thomas Taylor, sir," said Bennie, as he sank back, trembling, on the bench.

3

The lamp dropped from Jack Rennie's hand, and lay smoking at his feet. His huge frame seemed to have shrunk by at least a quarter of its size; and for many minutes he sat, silent and motionless, seeing as little of the objects around him as did the blind boy at his side.

At last he roused himself, picked up his lamp, and rose to his feet.

"Well, lad, Bennie, I mus' be a-goin'; good-by till ye. Will the brither come for ye?"

"Oh, yes!" answered Bennie, "Tom al'ays stops for me; he aint come up from the foot yet, but he'll come."

Rennie turned away, then turned back again.

"Whaur's the lamp?" he asked; "have ye no licht?"

"No; I don't ever have any. It wouldn't be any good to me, you know."

|24|

Once more the man started down the heading, but, after he had gone a short distance, a thought seemed to strike him, and he came back to where Bennie was still sitting.

"Lad, I thocht to tell ye; ye s'all go to the city wi' your eyes. I ha' money to sen' ye, an' ye s'all go. I—I—knew—the father, lad."

Before Bennie could express his surprise and gratitude, he felt a strong hand laid gently on his shoulder, and a rough, bearded face pressed for a moment against his own, and then his strange visitor was gone.

Down the heading the retreating footsteps echoed, their sound swallowed up at last in the distance; and up at Bennie's doorway silence reigned.

For a long time the boy sat, pondering the meaning of the strange man's words and conduct. But the more he thought about it the less able was he to understand it. Perhaps Tom could explain it, though; yes, he would tell Tom about it. Then it occurred to him that it was long past time|25| for Tom to come up from the foot with his last trip for the day. It was strange, too, that the men should all go out together that way; he didn't understand it. But if Tom would only come—

He rose and walked down the heading a little way; then he turned and went up through the door and along the airway; then he came back to his bench again, and sat down.

He was sure Tom would come; Tom had never disappointed him yet, and he knew he would not disappoint him for the world if he could help it. He knew, too, that it was long after quitting-time, and there hadn't been a sound, that he could hear, in the mine for an hour, though he had listened carefully.

After a while he began to grow nervous; the stillness became oppressive; he could not endure it. He determined to try to find the way out by himself. He had walked to the foot of the slope alone once, the day Tom was sick, and he thought he could do it again.

So he made sure that his door was|26| tightly closed, then he took his dinner-pail, and started bravely down the heading, striking the rails of the mine car-track on each side with his cane as he went along, to guide him.

Sometimes he would stop and listen, for a moment, if, perchance, he might hear Tom coming to meet him, or, possibly, some belated laborer going out from another part of the mine; then, hearing nothing, he would trudge on again.

After a long time spent thus, he thought he must be near the foot of the slope; he knew he had walked far enough to be there. He was tired, too, and sat down on the rail to rest. But he did not sit there long; he could not bear the silence, it was too depressing, and after a very little while he arose and walked on. The caps in the track grew higher; once he stumbled over one of them and fell, striking his side on the rail. He was in much pain for a few minutes; then he recovered and went on more carefully, lifting his feet high with every step, and reaching ahead with his cane. But his progress was very slow.

|27|

Then there came upon him the sensation of being in a strange place. It did not seem like the heading along which he went to and from his daily work. He reached out with his cane upon each side, and touched nothing. Surely, there was no place in the heading so wide as that.

But he kept on.

By-and-by he became aware that he was going down a steep incline. The echoes of his footsteps had a hollow sound, as though he were in some wide, open space, and his cane struck one, two, three, props in succession. Then he knew he was somewhere in a chamber; and knew, too, that he was lost.

He sat down, feeling weak and faint, and tried to think. He remembered that, at a point in the heading about two-thirds of the way to the foot, a passage branched off to the right, crossed under the slope, and ran out into the southern part of the mine, where he had never been. He thought he must have turned into this cross-heading, and followed it, and if he had, it would be hard indeed to tell where[28] he now was. He did not know whether to go on or to turn back.

Perhaps it would be better, after all, to sit still until help should come, though it might be hours, or even days, before any one would find him.

Then came a new thought. What would Tom do? Tom would not know where he had gone; he would never think of looking for him away off here; he would go up the heading to the door, and not finding him there, would think that his brother had already gone home. But when he knew that Bennie was not at home, he would surely come back to the mine to search for him; he would come down the slope; maybe he was, at that very moment, at the foot; maybe Tom would hear him if he should call, "Tom! O Tom!"

The loudest thunder-burst could not have been more deafening to the frightened child than the sound of his own voice, as it rang out through the solemn stillness of the mine, and was hurled back to his ears by the solid masses of rock and coal that closed in around him.

[29]

A thousand echoes went rattling down the wide chambers and along the narrow galleries, and sent back their ghosts to play upon the nervous fancy of the frightened child. He would not have shouted like that again if his life had depended on it.

Then silence fell upon him; silence like a pall—oppressive, mysterious and awful silence, in which he could almost hear the beating of his own heart. He could not endure that. He grasped his cane again and started on, searching for a path, stumbling over caps, falling sometimes, but on and on, though never so slowly; on and on until, faint and exhausted, he sank down upon the damp floor of the mine, with his face in his hands, and wept, in silent agony, like the lost child that he was.

Lost, indeed, with those miles and miles of black galleries opening and winding and crossing all around him, and he, lying prostrate and powerless, alone in the midst of that desolation.

[30]

CHAPTER II.
THE BURNED BREAKER.

For a long time Bennie lay there, pitifully weeping. Then, away off somewhere in the mine, he heard a noise. He lifted his head. By degrees the noise grew louder; then it sounded almost like footsteps. Suppose it were some one coming; suppose it were Tom! The light of hope flashed up in Bennie's breast with the thought.

But the sound ceased, the stillness settled down more profoundly than before, and about the boy's heart the fear and loneliness came creeping back. Was it possible that the noise was purely imaginary?

Suddenly, tripping down the passages, bounding from the walls, echoing through the chambers, striking faintly, but, oh, how[31] sweetly, upon Bennie's ears, came the well-known call,—

"Ben-nie-e-e-e!"

The sound died away in a faint succession of echoing *e*'s.

Bennie sprang to his feet with a cry.

"Tom! Tom! Tom, here I am."

Before the echoes of his voice came back to him they were broken by the sound of running feet, and down the winding galleries came Tom, as fast as his lamp and his legs would take him, never stopping till he and Bennie were in one another's arms.

"Bennie, it was my fault!" exclaimed Tom. "Patsy Donnelly told me you went out with Sandy McCulloch while I was up at the stables; an' I went way home, an' Mommie said you hadn't been there, an' I came back to find you, an' I went up to your door an' you wasn't there, an' I called an' called, an' couldn't hear no answer; an' then I thought maybe you'd tried to come out alone, an' got off in the cross headin' an' got lost, an'"—

Tom stopped from sheer lack of breath, and Bennie sobbed out,—

[32]

"I did, I did get lost an' scared, an'—an'—O Tom, it was awful!"

The thought of what he had experienced unnerved Bennie again, and, still holding Tom's hand, he sat down on the floor of the mine and wept aloud.

"There, Bennie, don't cry!" said Tom, soothingly; "don't cry! You're found now. Come, jump up an' le's go home; Mommie'll be half-crazy." It was touching to see the motherly way in which this boy of fourteen consoled and comforted his weaker brother, and helped him again to his feet. With his arm around the blind boy's waist, Tom led him down, through the chambers, out into the south heading, and so to the foot of the slope.

It was not a great distance; Bennie's progress had been so slow that, although he had, as he feared, wandered off by the cross heading into the southern part of the mine, he had not been able to get very far away.

At the foot of the slope they stopped to rest, and Bennie told about the strange man who had talked with him at the doorway.[33] Tom could give no explanation of the matter, except that the man must have been one of the strikers. The meaning of his strange conduct he could no more understand than could Bennie.

It was a long way up the slope, and for more than half the distance it was very steep; like climbing up a ladder. Many times on the upward way the boys stopped to rest. Always when he heard Bennie's breathing grow hard and laborious, Tom would complain of being himself tired, and they would turn about and sit for a few moments on a tie, facing down the slope.

Out at last into the quiet autumn night! Bennie breathed a long sigh of relief when he felt the yielding soil under his feet and the fresh air in his face.

Ah! could he but have seen the village lights below him, the glory of the sky and the jewelry of stars above him, and the half moon slipping up into the heavens from its hiding-place beyond the heights of Campbell's Ledge, he would, indeed, have known how sweet and beautiful the upper earth is, even with the veil of night across[34] it, compared with the black recesses of the mine.

It was fully a mile to the boys' home; but, with light hearts and willing feet, they soon left the distance behind them, and reached the low-roofed cottage, where the anxious mother waited in hope and fear for the coming of her children.

"Here we are, Mommie!" shouted Tom, as he came around the corner and saw her standing on the doorstep in the moonlight watching. Out into the road she ran then, and gathered her two boys into her arms, kissed their grimy, coal-blackened faces, and listened to their oft-interrupted story, with smiles and with tears, as she led them to her house.

But Tom stopped at the door and turned back.

"I promised Sandy McCulloch," he said, "to go over an' tell him if I found Bennie. He said he'd wait up for me, an' go an' help me hunt him up if I came back without him. It's only just over beyond the breaker; it won't take twenty minutes, an' Sandy'll be expectin' me."

[35]

And without waiting for more words, the boy started off on a run.

It was already past ten o'clock, and he had not had a mouthful of supper, but that was nothing in consideration of the fact that Sandy had been good to him, and would have helped him, and was, even now, waiting for him. So, with a light and grateful heart, he hurried on.

He passed beyond the little row of cottages, of which his mother's was one, over the hill by a foot-path, and then along the mine car-track to the breaker. Before him the great building loomed up, like some huge castle of old, cutting its outlines sharply against the moon-illumined sky, and throwing a broad black shadow for hundreds of feet to the west.

6

Through the shadow went Tom, around by the engine-room, where the watchman's light was glimmering faintly through the grimy window; out again into the moonlight, up, by a foot-path, to the summit of another hill, along by another row of darkened dwellings, to a cottage where a light was still burning, and there he stopped.

[36]

The door opened before he reached it, and a man in shirt-sleeves stepped out and hailed him:

"Is that you, Tom? An' did ye find Bennie?"

"Yes, Sandy. I came to tell you we just got home. Found him down in the south chambers; he tried to come out alone, an' got lost. So I'll not need you, Sandy, with the same thanks as if I did, an' good-night to you!"

"Good-nicht till ye, Tom! I'm glad the lad's safe wi' the mither. Tom," as the boy turned away, "ye'll not be afeard to be goin' home alone?"

Tom laughed.

"Do I looked scared, Sandy? Give yourself no fear for me; I'm afraid o' naught."

Before Sandy turned in at his door, Tom had disappeared below the brow of the hill. The loose gravel rolled under his feet as he hurried down, and once, near the bottom, he slipped and fell.

As he rose, he was astonished to see the figure of a man steal carefully along in[37] the shadow of the breaker, and disappear around the corner by the engine-room.

Tom went down cautiously into the shadow, and stopped for a moment in the track by the loading-place to listen. He thought he heard a noise in there; something that sounded like the snapping of dry twigs.

The next moment a man came out from under that portion of the breaker, with his head turned back over his shoulder, muttering, as he advanced toward Tom,—

"There, Mike, that's the last job o' that kind I'll do for all the secret orders i' the warl'. They put it on to me because I've got no wife nor childer, nor ither body to cry their eyes oot, an' I get i' the prison for it. But I've had the hert o' me touched the day, Mike, an' I canna do the like o' this again; it's the las' time, min' ye, the las' time I—Mike!—why, that's no' Mike! Don't ye speak, lad! don't ye whusper! don't ye stir!"

The man stepped forward, a very giant in size, with a great beard floating on his breast, and laid his brawny hands on[38] Tom's shoulders with a grip that made the lad wince.

Tom did not stir; he was too much frightened for one thing, too much astonished for another. For, before the man had finished speaking, there appeared under the loading-place in the breaker a little flickering light, and the light grew into a flame, and the flame curled around the coal-black timbers, and sent up little red tongues to lick the cornice of the long, low roof. Tom was so astounded that he could not speak, even if he had dared. But this giant was standing over him, gripping his shoulders in a painful clutch, and saying to him, in a voice of emphasis and determination,—

"Do ye see me, lad? Do ye hear me? Then I say to ye, tell a single soul what ye've seen here the night, an' the life o' ye's not worth the dust i' the road. Whusper a single word o' it, an' the Molly Maguires 'll tak' terrible revenge o' ye'! Noo, then, to your home! Rin! an' gin ye turn your head or speak, ye s'all wish ye'd 'a' been i' the midst o' the fire instead."

[39]

With a vigorous push, he sent Tom from him at full speed down the track.

But the boy had not gone far before the curiosity that overtook Lot's wife came upon him, and he turned and looked. He was just in time to see and hear the sleepy watchman open the door of the engine-room, run out, give one startled look at the flames as they went creeping up the long slant of roof, and then make the still night echo with his cry of "Fire!"

Before twenty minutes had passed, the surrounding hills were alive with people who had come to look upon the burning breaker.

The spectacle was a grand one.

For many minutes the fire played about in the lower part of the building, among the pockets and the screens, and dashed up against the base of the shaft-tower like lapping waves. Then the small square windows, dotting the black surface of the breaker here and

7

there up its seventy feet of height, began to redden and to glow with the mounting flames behind them; a column of white smoke broke from the|40|topmost cornice, little red tongues went creeping up to the very pinnacle of the tower, and then from the highest point of all a great column of fire shot far up toward the onlooking stars, and the whole gigantic building was a single body of roaring, wavering flame.

It burned rapidly and brilliantly, and soon after midnight there was but a mass of charred ruins covering the ground where once the breaker stood.

There was little that could be saved; the cars in the loading-place, the tools in the engine-room, some loose lumber, and the household effects from a small dwelling-house near by; that was all. But among the many men who helped to save this little, none labored with such energetic effort, such daring zeal, such superhuman strength, as the huge-framed, big-bearded man they called Jack Rennie.

The strike had become general. The streets of the mining towns were filled with idle, loitering men and boys. The drinking|41| saloons drove a brisk business, and the merchants feared disaster. Tom had not told any one as yet of his adventure at the breaker on the night of the fire. He knew that he ought to disclose his secret; indeed, he felt a pressing duty upon him to do so in order that the crime might be duly punished. But the secret order of Molly Maguires was a terror in the coal regions in those days; the torch, the pistol, and the knife were the instruments with which it carried out its desperate decrees, and Tom was absolutely afraid to whisper a word of what he knew, even to his mother or to Bennie.

But one day the news went out that Jack Rennie had been arrested, charged with setting fire to the Valley Breaker; and soon afterward a messenger came to the house of the Widow Taylor, saying that Tom was wanted immediately in Wilkesbarre at the office of Lawyer Pleadwell.

Tom answered this summons gladly, as it might possibly afford a means by which he would be compelled to tell what he knew about the fire, with the least responsibility|42| resting on him for the disclosure. But he resolved that, in no event, would he speak any thing but the truth.

After he was dressed and brushed to the satisfaction of his careful mother, Tom went with the messenger to the railroad station, and the fast train soon brought them into the city of Wilkesbarre, the county town of Luzerne County.

On one of the streets radiating from the court-house square, they stopped before a dingy-looking door on which was fastened a sign reading: "James G. Pleadwell, Attorney-at-Law."

Tom was taken, first, into the outer room of the law-offices, where a man sat at a table writing, and two or three other men, evidently miners, were talking together in a corner; and then, after a few moments, the door into an inner apartment was opened and he was called in there. This room was more completely furnished than the outer one; there was a carpet on the floor, and there were pictures on the walls; also there were long shelves full of books, all bound alike in|43| leather, all with red labels near the tops and black labels near the bottoms of their backs.

At the farther side of the room sat a short, slim, beardless man, with pale face and restless eyes, whom Tom recognized as having been in the mine with the visiting strikers the day Bennie was lost; and by a round centre table sat Lawyer Pleadwell, short and stout, with bristly mustache and a stubby nose on which rested a pair of gold-rimmed eye-glasses.

As Tom entered the room, the lawyer regarded him closely, and waving his hand towards an easy chair, he said,—

"Be seated, my lad. Your name is—a'—let me see"—

"Tom—Thomas Taylor, sir," answered the boy.

"Well, Tom, you saw the fire at the Valley Breaker?"

"Yes, sir," said Tom; "I guess I was the first one 'at saw it."

"So I have heard," said the lawyer, slowly; then, after a pause,—

"Tom have you told to any one what|44| you saw, or whom you saw at the moment of the breaking out of that fire?"

8

"I have not, sir," answered Tom, wondering how the lawyer knew he had seen any one.

"Do you expect, or desire, to disclose your knowledge?"

"I do," said Tom; "I ought to a' told before; I meant to a' told, but I didn't dare. I'd like to tell now."

Tom was growing bold; he felt that he had kept the secret long enough and that, now, it must out.

Lawyer Pleadwell twirled his glasses thoughtfully for a few moments, then placed them deliberately on his nose, and turned straight to Tom.

"Well, Tom," he said, "we may as well be plain with you. I represent Jack Rennie, who is charged with firing this breaker, and Mr. Carolan here is officially connected with the order of Molly Maguires, in pursuance of whose decree the deed is supposed to have been done. We have known, for some time, that a boy was present when the breaker was fired. Last|45| night we learned that you were that boy. Now, what we want of you is simply this: to keep your knowledge to yourself. This will be to your own advantage as well as for the benefit of others. Will you do it?"

To Tom, the case had taken on a new aspect. Instead of being, as he had supposed, in communication with those who desired to punish the perpetrators of the crime, he found himself in the hands of the prisoner's friends. But his Scotch stubbornness came to the rescue, and he replied,—

"I can't do it, sir; it wasn't right to burn the breaker, an' the man 'at done it ought to go to jail for it."

Lawyer Pleadwell inserted a thumb into the arm-hole of his vest, and poised his glasses carefully in his free hand. He was preparing to argue the case with Tom.

"Suppose," said he, "you were a miner, as you hope to be, as your father was before you; and a brutal and soulless corporation, having reduced your wages to the starvation-point, while its vaults were|46| gorged with money, should kick you, like a dog, out of their employ, when you humbly asked them for enough to keep body and soul together. Suppose you knew that the laws were made for the rich and against the poor, as they are, and that your only redress, and a speedy one, would be to spoil the property of your persecutors till they came to treat you like a human being, with rights to be respected, as they surely would, for they fear nothing so much as the torch; would you think it right for a fellow-workman to deliver you up to their vengeance and fury for having taught them such a lesson?"

The lawyer placed his glasses on his nose, and leaned forward, eagerly, towards Tom.

The argument was not without its effect. Tom had long been led to believe that corporations were tyrannical monsters. But the boy's inherent sense of right and wrong was proof against even this specious plea.

"All the same," he said, "I can't make out 'at it's right to burn a breaker. Why,"|47| he continued, "you might say the same thing if it'd 'a been murder."

Pleadwell saw that he was on the wrong track with this clear-headed boy.

"Well," he said, settling back in his chair, "if peaceful persuasion will not avail, I trust you are prepared, in case of disclosure, to meet whatever the Molly Maguires have in store for you?"

"Yes," answered Tom, boldly, "I am. I've been afraid of 'em, an' that's what's kept me from tellin'; but I won't be a coward any more; they can do what they're a mind to with me."

The lawyer was in a quandary, and Carolan shot angry glances at Tom. Here was a lad who held Jack Rennie's fate in his hands, and whom neither fear nor persuasion could move. What was to be done?

Pleadwell motioned to Carolan, and they rose and left the room together; while Tom sat, with tumultuously beating heart, but with constantly increasing resolution.

The men were gone but a few moments,|48| and came back with satisfied looks on their faces.

"I have learned," said the lawyer, addressing Tom, in a voice laden with apparent sympathy, "that you have a younger brother who is blind. That is a sad affliction."

"Yes, indeed it is," replied Tom; "yes, indeed!"

9

"I have learned, also, that there is a possibility of cure, if the eyes are subjected to proper and timely treatment."

"Yes, that's what a doctor told us."

"What a blessing it would be if sight could be restored to him! what a delight! What rejoicing there would be in your little household, would there not?"

"Oh, indeed there would!" cried Tom, "oh, indeed! It's what we're a-thinkin' of al'ays; it's what I pray for every night, sir. We've been a-tryin' to save money enough to do it, but it's slow a-gettin' it, it's awful slow."

"A—how much"—Lawyer Pleadwell paused, and twirled his eye-glasses thoughtfully—"how much would it cost, Tom?"

[49]

"Only a hundred dollars, sir; that's what the doctor said."

Another pause; then, with great deliberation,—

"Tom, suppose my friend here should see fit to place in your hands, to-day, the sum of one hundred dollars, to be used in your brother's behalf; could you return the favor by keeping to yourself the knowledge you possess concerning the origin of the fire at the breaker?"

The hot blood surged up into Tom's face, his heart pounded like a hammer against his breast, his head was in a whirl.

A hundred dollars! and sight for Bennie! No lies to be told—only to keep quiet—and sight for Bennie! Would it be very wrong? But, oh, to think of Bennie in the joy of seeing! The temptation was terrible. Stronger, less affectionate natures than Tom's might well have yielded.

[50]

CHAPTER III.
THE UNQUIET CONSCIENCE.

And Tom yielded.

The whisperings of conscience were drowned in the anticipation of Bennie's joy. The fear of personal violence would not have conquered him; neither would the fallacious argument of compensation by destruction have done so. But that vision of Bennie, with eyes that could look into his eyes, with eyes that could see the houses and the breakers, the trees and the birds and the flowers, that could even see the far-off stars in the sky at night,—that was the vision that crowded out from Tom's mind the sharp distinction between right and wrong, and delivered him over wholly to the tempter.

But he felt the shame of it, nevertheless, as he answered, in a choking voice, at last,—

[51]

"Yes, I could. A hundred dollars 'd give sight to Bennie. I wouldn't lie for it, but I'll keep still for it."

Lawyer Pleadwell doubled up his glasses, slipped them into a morocco case, and slipped the case into his vest-pocket. His object was accomplished.

"Tom," he said, "you're a wise lad. If you keep on in this way, you'll make a lawyer; and a lawyer, with so evenly balanced a conscience as yours, will be a credit to the profession."

Tom was not quite sure whether this was intended for a compliment or not, so he simply said, "Yes, sir."

Pleadwell reached across the table for his high silk hat, motioned to Carolan to follow him, and went out, saying to Tom as he went,—

"You stay here and amuse yourself; we'll be back shortly."

Tom sat there alone quite still. His mind was in a tumult. Is it right? Is it *right?* Some unseen presence kept crowding the question in upon him.

What would Bennie say to it?

[52]

What would Mommie say to it?

Yet there were no lies to be told; he was simply to hold his tongue.

10

But was it not shielding a criminal from just punishment? Was it not virtually selling his honor for money? Would it not be better, after all, to take back his promise, to do his duty fearlessly, and to work and wait, patiently and with a clear conscience, for means to accomplish the desire of his heart for Bennie?

He was just getting into a state of painful indecision when Carolan came in alone, and closed the door carefully behind him. Without saying a word, he handed to Tom, one by one, ten crisp, new ten-dollar bills. The boy had never in his life before seen so much money at one time. To hold it was like a scene in a fairy story; to own it was to be rich beyond belief. The whispers of conscience were again stilled in the novelty of possessing wealth with which such blessings might be bought.

Tom took the money, folded it awkwardly, and placed it in the inside pocket of his vest. Carolan looked on with apparent[53] satisfaction; then went and seated himself in the chair he had formerly occupied, without having uttered a word.

This man was a marked character in the anthracite coal region twenty years ago. He was known among the miners as "Silent Mike," was credited with much native ability and sharpness, and was generally believed to be at the head, in the anthracite region, of the secret order of Molly Maguires. He was always shrewd enough not to implicate himself in any lawlessness. The fact that he so controlled the organization as to meet his personal ends caused it, eventually, to be split with internal dissensions. Then, as a new reign of law and order came in, and as organized labor began to base itself on higher principles, and to work out its problem with less of vengeance and more of justice, the order gradually passed out of existence.

Thinking there was nothing more to be said or done, Tom rose to go; but just then Pleadwell entered, laid his silk hat carefully on the table, and motioned to him to be seated. Having taken his eye-glasses[54] from their case and adjusted them carefully on his nose, he said to Tom,—

"It will not be wise for you to make any large expenditures of money for any purpose until after the trial; and in the mean time it will be absolutely unsafe for you to disclose to any one the fact of your having money or the means by which it was obtained. Your own discretion will teach you this. You understand me, do you not?"

Tom nodded, and Pleadwell continued:

"There is one thing more that I desire to speak of: I have heard that when you reached the foot of the hill on the night the breaker was burned, you saw a man come from near the point where the fire broke out, pass by you in the shadow of the building, and disappear around the corner by the engine-room. Is this true?"

"Yes, sir."

"What kind of a looking man was this? Describe him."

"He was a short man," Tom replied, "kind o' slim, an' he didn't have any whiskers"— a sudden thought seemed[55] to strike the boy, and looking for a moment earnestly at Carolan, and then pointing his finger at him, he exclaimed,—

"Why, he looked just like—just like him!"

Carolan smiled grimly, but Pleadwell laughed aloud.

"Well, Tom," he said, "we shall not ask you to tell whom he looks like, but if I should require your presence at the trial, and should call you to the witness-stand, you would have no objection, I presume, to giving a description of the man you saw pass by you in the shadow of the breaker, just as you have described him to me?"

"No," replied Tom, "not so long as it's true."

"Oh, I should expect you to say nothing that is not strictly true," said Pleadwell. "I would not allow a witness of mine to tell a lie. Well, then, you are to be in the court-room here a week from next Tuesday morning at nine o'clock. Do you understand?"

"Yes, sir."

"Carolan, put Thomas Taylor's name on[56] that subpœna. You will consider yourself subpœnaed, Tom. Now," taking a heavy gold watch from his fob-pocket and glancing at it, "you will have just time to catch the train north." Then stepping to the door between the two rooms, and throwing it open, he said, "Harris, go to the station with this boy, buy his ticket, and see that he gets the right train."

Harris was the young man who came down with Tom, and he and the boy were soon on the street together, walking briskly toward the station.

An hour earlier, when they were coming in, Tom had been very talkative and inquiring, but now his companion was able to get from him no more than a simple "yes" or "no," and that only in answer to questions.

Conversation was impossible to the boy, with his mind so crowded with perplexing doubts. He could not even take notice of the shop-windows, or of the life in the streets, but followed blindly along by the side of Harris. Somehow he felt as though he were walking under a heavy[57] weight, and that roll of money in his pocket seemed to be burning him where it rested against his breast. He imagined that the people he met looked at him suspiciously, as if they knew he had been bribed—*bribed*!

The word came into his mind so suddenly, and with such startling force, that he stopped still in the street, and only recovered himself when Harris turned and called to him.

They were just in time for the train.

Tom found a place in the corner of the car where he would be alone, and sat there thinking over what he had done, and trying to reason himself into justification of his conduct.

The conductor came along and punched his ticket, and looked at him so sharply that Tom wondered if he knew. But of course that was absurd. Then he tried to dismiss the matter from his mind altogether, and give his attention to what he could see from the car-window.

Outside a drizzling rain was beginning to fall on the brown fields and leafless trees,[58] and the autumn early twilight was fast deepening into darkness. It was very dismal and cheerless, and not at all the kind of outlook that could serve to draw Tom's mind from its task of self-contemplation. It was but a few minutes, therefore, before this controversy with himself was going on again, harder than before.

Somehow that strange word "bribed" kept haunting him. It sounded constantly in his ears. He imagined that the people in the cars were speaking it; that even the rhythmic rattle of the wheels upon the rails kept singing it to him with monotonous reiteration, "Bribed! *bribed*!"

Tom thought, as he hurried down the street in the gathering darkness, out upon the plank walk, and up the long hill toward home, that he had never been so unhappy in all his life before. It was strange, too, for he had so often dreamed of the great joy he should feel when the coveted hundred dollars had been saved.

Well, he had it now, every cent of it, rolled up and tucked safely away in the[59] pocket of his vest; but instead of happiness, it had brought misery.

For the first time within his memory, the thought of meeting his mother and his brother gave him no pleasure. He would not tell them about the money that night at any rate; he had decided upon that. Indeed, he had almost concluded that it would be better that they should not know about it until after the trial. And then suppose they should not approve! He was aghast at the very thought.

But Tom was a brave lad, and he put on a bright face before these two, and told them of his trip to Wilkesbarre, and about what he had seen and heard,—about the law-office, about Pleadwell and Carolan, about every thing, indeed, but the bargain and the money.

He tried to eat his supper as if he enjoyed it, though every mouthful seemed about to choke him, and on the plea of being very tired, he went early to bed. There he lay half the night debating with his conscience, trying to make himself believe that he had done right, yet feeling[60] all the time that he had stooped to dishonor.

He went over in his mind the way in which he should break the news to Mommie and Bennie, and wondered how they would receive it; and always beating upon his brain, with a regular cadence that followed the pulsation of his heart, and with a monotonous rhythm that haunted him even after he had fallen into a troubled sleep, went that terrible word, *Bribed*!

The autumn days went by, and still the strike continued. There were no signs of resumption, no signs of compromise. On the contrary, the breach between the miners and the operators was growing daily wider. The burning of the Valley breaker and the arrest of

Jack Rennie had given rise to a bitterness of feeling between the two classes that hindered greatly an amicable settlement of their differences.

Acts of lawlessness were common, and it was apparent that but little provocation would be needed to bring on deeds of|61| violence of a desperate nature. The cry of want began to be heard, and, as the winter season was drawing near, suffering became more frequent among the improvident and the unfortunate.

The Taylor family saw coming the time when the pittance of twenty dollars that the boys had saved for Bennie must be drawn upon to furnish food and clothing for them all. Tom had tried to get work outside of the mines, but had failed; there were so many idle men and boys, and there was so little work to be done at that season of the year. But the district school was open, not far from his home, and Tom went there instead.

He was fond of books, and had studied much by himself. He could read very well indeed. He used to read aloud to Bennie a great deal, and during these days of enforced idleness the boys occupied much of their time in that way; finding their literature in copies of old newspapers which had been given to them, and in a few old books which had belonged to their father.

|62|

Indian Summer came late that year, but it was very fair. It lingered day after day, with its still air, its far-sounding echoes, its hazy light and its smoky distances; and the brooding spirit of nature's quiet rested down, for a brief but beautiful season, about the unquiet spirits of men.

On the afternoon of one of its most charming days, Tom and Bennie sauntered out, hand in hand, as they always went, to where the hill, south of their little mining village, rose like a huge, upturned bowl, sloping downward from its summit to every point of the compass. Over in the little valley to the south lay the ruins of the burned breaker, still untouched; and off upon the other side, one could see the sparkling Susquehanna far up into the narrow valley where its waters sweep around the base of Campbell's Ledge; across to the blue mountains on the west; and down the famous valley of Wyoming, with its gray stone monument in the middle distance, until the eastern hills crept in to intercept the view.

It was a dreamy day, and a day fit for|63| dreams, and when the boys reached the summit of the hill, Tom lay down upon the warm sod, and silently looked away to the haze-wrapped mountains, while Bennie sat by his side, and pictured to his mind the view before him, as Tom had described it to him many times, sitting in that very spot.

Poor Tom! These beautiful days had brought to him much perplexity of mind, much futile reasoning with his conscience, and much, very much, of silent suffering.

Lying there now, in the sunlight, with open eyes, he saw, in reality, no more of the beautiful scene before him than did blind Bennie at his side. He was thinking of the trial, now only three days distant, of what he should be called upon to do and to say, and of how, after it was all over, he must tell Mommie and Bennie about the hundred dollars.

Ah, there was the trouble! he could see his way clearly enough until it should come to that; but how should he ever be able to tell to these two a thing of which he tried|64| to be proud, but of which, after all, he felt guilty and ashamed?

Then, what would they say to him? Would they praise him for his devotion to Bennie, and for his cleverness in having grasped an opportunity? Or would they grieve over his lack of manly firmness and his loss of boyish honor? Alas! the more he thought of it, the more he feared that they would sorrow rather than rejoice.

But an idea came to Tom, as he lay there, thinking the matter over; the idea that perhaps he could learn what Bennie's mind would be on the subject, without exciting any suspicion therein of what had actually occurred. He resolved to try.

He hardly knew how best to approach the matter, but, after some consideration, he turned to Bennie and said,—

"Bennie, do you s'pose Jack Rennie act'ally set fire to that breaker?"

"I shouldn't wonder a bit, Tom," replied Bennie; "those 'at know, him says he's dreadful bad. 'Taint so much worse to burn a breaker than 'tis to burn a shaft-house, an' they say he act'ally did burn a|65| shaft-house up at Hyde Park, only they couldn't prove it on him."

13

"Well, s'pose you'd 'a' seen—s'pose you could see, you know, Bennie—an' s'pose you'd 'a' seen Jack Rennie set fire to that breaker; would you tell on him?"

"Yes, I would," said Bennie, resolutely, "if I thought he'd never get punished for it 'less I did tell on him."

"Well, don't you think," continued Tom, reflectively, "'at that'd be sidin' with the wealthy *clapitulist*, against the poor laborer, who ain't got no other way to get even justice for himself, except to make the rich*corpurations* afraid of him, that way?"

Tom was using Pleadwell's argument, not because he believed in it himself, but simply to see how Bennie would meet it.

Bennie met it by saying,—

"Well, I don't care; I don't b'lieve it's *ever* right to burn up any thing 'at belongs to anybody else; an' if I saw any one a-doin' it, I'd tell on him if"—Bennie hesitated a moment, and Tom looked up eagerly—"if I wasn't afraid o' the Molly|66| Maguires. Jack Rennie's a Molly, you know."

"But *wouldn't* you be afraid of 'em? s'pose one of 'em should come to you an' say, 'Ben Taylor, if you tell on Jack, we'll put out your'—I mean 'cut off your tongue.' What'd you do?"

Bennie thought a moment.

"Well, I b'lieve I'd tell on him, anyway; an' then I'd get a pistol, an' I wouldn't let no Molly get nearer to me'n the muzzle of it."

In spite of his great anxiety, Tom laughed at the picture of weak, blind little Bennie holding a crowd of outlaws at bay, with a cocked revolver in his hand. But he felt that he was not getting at the real question very fast, so he tried again.

"Well, Bennie, s'pose you'd 'a' seen him start that fire, an' he'd 'a' knowed it, an' he'd 'a' said to you, 'Ben Taylor, if you ever tell on me, I'll burn your Mommie's house down, an' I'll most kill your brother Tom!' *then* what'd you do?"

Bennie hesitated. This was more of a poser.

|67|

"Well," he answered, at last, "if I'd 'a' b'lieved he'd 'a' done what he said—I don't know—I guess I'd—well, maybe, if I didn't have to tell any lie, I just wouldn't say any thing."

Tom's spirits rose; he felt that a great point was gained. Here was a matter in which Bennie would have been even less firm than he himself had been. Now was the time to come directly to the issue, to ask the final question.

Tom braced himself to the task. He tried to speak naturally and carelessly, but there was a strange shortness of breath, and a huskiness in his voice which he could not control; he could only hope that Bennie would not notice it.

"Well, then, s'pose—just s'pose, you know—that *I'd* seen Jack Rennie set fire to the breaker, an' 'at he knew I was goin' to tell on him, an' 'at he'd 'a' said to me, 'Tom, you got a blind brother Bennie, ain't you?' an' I'd 'a' said, 'Yes,' an' he'd 'a' said, 'What'll it cost to get Bennie's sight for him?' an' I'd 'a' said, 'Oh, maybe a hundred dollars,' an' he'd 'a' said, 'Here, Tom,|68| here's a hundred dollars; you go an' get Bennie's eyes cured; an' don't you say any thin' about my settin' that fire.' What—what'd you 'a' done if you'd 'a' been me?"

Tom raised himself to a sitting posture, and leaned toward Bennie, with flushed face and painful expectancy in his eyes.

He knew that for him Bennie's answer meant either a return to a measure of the old happiness, or a plunging into deeper misery.

The blind boy rose to his feet and stood for a moment as if lost in thought. Then he turned his sightless eyes to Tom, and said, very slowly and distinctly,—

"If you'd 'a' took it, Tom, an' if you'd 'a' used it to cure me with, an' I'd 'a' known it, an' I'd 'a' got my sight, I don't believe—I don't believe I should ever 'a' wanted to look at you, Tom, or wanted you to see me; I'd 'a' been so 'shamed o' both of us."

|69|

CHAPTER IV.
THE TRIAL.

14

Tom turned his head away, and covered his face with his hands. This was cruel. For the first time in his life, he was glad Bennie could not see him. But he felt that it was necessary for him to say something, so he stammered out,—

"Well, I was only just s'posin', you know. Course, no honest fellow'd do that; but if they'll only get to work again, we won't ask anybody for any hunderd dollars. We'll earn it."

The beauty of the autumn day died slowly out, and the narrow crescent of the new moon, hanging over the tops of the far western hills, shone dimly through the purple haze. Sadly and with few words the two boys went their homeward way. A great burden of regret and remorse[70] rested upon Tom's heart, and the shadow of it fell upon the heart of his blind brother.

Poor, poor Tom! He knew not what to do. He could never use the money now for Bennie, and he would not use it for himself. It had occurred to him once to take the money back to Pleadwell, and seek to be released from his agreement. But a little thought had convinced him that this would be useless; that the money would not be received; that, having accepted a bribe, he had placed himself in the power of those who had given it to him, and that any wavering on his part, much more any violation of his agreement, would bring down vengeance and punishment on himself, and trouble and disgrace on those who were dear to him.

"Oh, why," he asked himself, in bitter thought, "why did I ever take the money?"

Tom's mother attributed his melancholy to lack of work and loss of earnings. She knew how his heart was set on laying up money to send Bennie away, and how impatient he became at any delay in the progress[71] of his scheme. So she talked to him very cheerfully, and made delicate little dishes to tempt his appetite, and when the morning for the trial came, and Tom started for the train to go to Wilkesbarre, dressed in his best clothes, and with the hated hundred dollars burning in his pocket, she kissed him good-by with a smile on her face. She bade him many times to be very careful about the cars, and said to him, at parting, "Whatever tha says to thee, lad, tell the truth; whatever tha does to thee, tell the truth; fear to look no man i' the eye; be good an' honest wi' yoursel', an' coom back to Mommie an' Bennie, when it's ower, hearty an' weel."

Sandy McCulloch went down with Tom on the train, and together they walked from the station to the Court House. There were many people standing about in the Court-House Square, and in the corridors of the building, and the court-room itself was nearly full when Tom and Sandy entered it. They found vacant places on one of the rear benches, but, as the seats were all graded down on a sloping floor to[72] the bar, they could see without difficulty all that was being done.

Tom had never been in a court-room before, and he looked with much interest at the judges on the bench, at the lawyers chatting pleasantly in the bar, at the entry and departure of the grand jury, and at the officious constables, each with his staff of office, who kept order in the court-room.

There were some motions and arguments which Tom could not understand, being made by the attorneys; the clerk read some lists in a weak voice, and the time of the court was thus occupied until toward noon.

By and by there was a slight bustle at the side door, to the right of the judges' bench, and the sheriff and his deputy entered with Jack Rennie.

Head and shoulders above those who accompanied him, his heavily bearded face somewhat pale from confinement, and stooping rather more than usual, he moved slowly across the crowded bar, in full view of all the people in the room, to a seat by the side of his counsel.

[73]

The instant Tom's eyes rested on him he recognized him as the man who had threatened him at the breaker on the night of the fire. The buzz of excitement, occasioned by the entrance of the prisoner, subsided, and the voice of the presiding judge sounded distinctly through the room:

"Commonwealth against Jack Rennie. Arson. Are you ready for trial?"

"We are, your Honor," replied the district attorney, rising to his feet and advancing to the clerk's desk.

15

"Very well," said the judge. "Arraign the prisoner."

Rennie was directed to stand up, and the district attorney read, in a clear voice, the indictment, which charged that the defendant "did, on the eighteenth day of November last passed, feloniously, wilfully and maliciously set fire to, burn and consume, a certain building, to wit: a coal-breaker, the same being the property of a certain body corporate known by the style and title of 'The Valley Coal Company;' by reason of which setting fire to, burning[74] and consuming, a certain dwelling-house, also the property of the said Valley Coal Company, and being within the curtilage of said coal-breaker, was also burned and consumed; contrary to the form of the act of the General Assembly, in such case made and provided, and against the peace and dignity of the Commonwealth of Pennsylvania."

Rennie stood, listening intently to the reading of the indictment. When the question was put:

"What say you,—guilty, or not guilty?" he replied, in a deep, chest voice,—

"If I be guilty, ye ha' but to prove it."

"Make your plea, sir!" said the judge severely. "Guilty, or not guilty?"

"Then I'll plead no' guilty. No mon's guilty till he's proved guilty."

Rennie resumed his seat, and the court was soon afterward adjourned for the noon recess.

In the afternoon the selecting of jurors in the case against Rennie began.

The first one called was a miner. One could tell that by the blue powder-marks[75] on his face, and that he was of Irish nativity could be detected by the rich brogue that escaped his lips. He was "passed" by the Commonwealth, and the clerk of the court recited the formula:

"Juror, look upon the prisoner. Prisoner, look upon the juror. What say you,— challenge, or no challenge?"

"Swear the juror to 'true answers make,'" said Attorney Pleadwell.

The man was sworn.

"Where do you live?" inquired the lawyer.

"Up on Shanty Hill, sorr."

"That's definite. Anywhere near this breaker that was burned?"

"Oh, the matther of a mile belike, barrin' the time it'd take ye to walk to the track beyant."

"What's your occupation?"

"Occupation, is it? Yis, sorr; as good a charra̤ter as anny"—

"Oh, I mean what do you work at?"

"I'm a miner, sorr."

"Where do you work?"

"Faith, I worked for the Valley Breaker[76] Coal Company this tin years come next St. Patrick's day, may it plase the coort, an' bad 'cess to the man that burnt it, I say, an'"—

"Challenge!" interrupted Attorney Pleadwell, sharply.

A tipstaff hurried the challenged man from the witness-box, in a state of helpless bewilderment as to what it all meant, and another juror was called, a small, wiry man, chewing on a mouthful of tobacco. He was sworn on his *voir dire*, and the district attorney asked him,—

"Do you belong to an organization known as the Molly Maguires?"

"No, sir!" quickly responded the man, before Pleadwell could interpose an objection to the question.

The district attorney looked at the witness sharply for a moment, then consulted with Attorney Summons, who sat by his side as private counsel for the prosecution. They believed that the man had sworn falsely, in order to get on the jury in behalf of the defendant, and he was directed to stand aside.

[77]

The next juror called was a farmer from a remote part of the county, who had heard nothing about the fire until he arrived in town, and who displayed no prejudices. He was accepted by both sides as the first juror in the case.

16

So the selection went on, slowly and tediously, enlivened at times by an amusing candidate for the jury-box, or a tilt between counsel; and long before the "twelve good men and true" had all been selected and sworn, the early autumn night had fallen, and the flaring gas-jets lighted up the space about the bench and bar, leaving the remote corners of the court-room in uncertain shadow.

At six o'clock court was adjourned until the following morning, and Tom went, with Sandy McCulloch, to a small hotel on the outskirts of the city, where arrangements had been made to accommodate witnesses for the defence. Notwithstanding his anxiety of mind, Tom was hungry, and he ate a hearty supper and went early to bed.

But he could not sleep. The excitement[78] of the day had left his brain in a whirl, and he tossed restlessly about, going over in his mind what had already occurred, and thinking with grave apprehension of what to-morrow might bring forth. Through it all he still repeated one resolve: that whatever came he would not lie.

With this unsatisfactory compromise with his conscience on his mind, he fell at last into a troubled sleep.

When court was opened on the following morning, the court-room was more densely crowded with idle men than it had been on the previous day. The case against Rennie was taken up without delay. The district attorney made the opening address on behalf of the Commonwealth, doing little more than to outline the evidence to be presented by the prosecution.

The first witness called was a civil engineer, who presented a map showing the plan, location and surroundings of the burned breaker. Following him came two witnesses who detailed the progress of the fire as they had seen it, one of them being the watchman at the breaker, and the other[79] the occupant of the dwelling-house which had been burned.

A third witness testified to having seen Rennie at the fire shortly after it broke out, but did not know how long he had been there, nor where he came from; and still another swore that he had seen the defendant in a drinking-saloon in town, about half an hour before he heard the alarm of fire, and had noticed that he went away, in the direction of the breaker, in company with "Silent Mike."

Then came a witness who gave his name as Lewis G. Travers; a slightly built, but muscular man, of middle age, with sharp eyes and quiet manner.

"What is your occupation?" inquired the district attorney, after the man had been sworn.

"I am a detective."

"Do you know Jack Rennie, the defendant?"

"I do."

"Where did you last see him?"

"At a meeting, in Carbondale, of certain members of the order of Molly Maguires."
[80]

"Are you a member of that order?"

"I have been."

"Will you relate the circumstances attending your connection with it?"

The stillness in the court-room was marvellous. On many an expectant face were mingled expressions of hate and fear, as the witness, with calm deliberation, related the thrilling story of how he had worked as a common laborer in the mines, in order to gain a standing with the lawless miners, and of how he had then been admitted to the order of Molly Maguires, and had taken part in their deliberations.

As a member of the executive board, he had been present, he said, at a secret meeting held in Carbondale, at which, on account of the outspoken denunciation of the order, and the prompt dismissal of men belonging to it, by the owners of the Valley Breaker, it was resolved to visit them with vengeance, in the shape of fire; that Jack Rennie was selected to carry out the resolution, and that Rennie, being present, had registered a solemn oath to do the bidding of the order.
[81]

This was the substance of his testimony, and though the cross-examination, by Pleadwell, was sharp, rigid and severe, the effect of the evidence could not be broken.

17

At this point the Commonwealth rested. The case against Rennie had assumed a serious phase. Unless he could produce some strong evidence in his favor, his conviction was almost assured.

Pleadwell rose to open the case for the defence. After some general remarks on the unfairness of the prosecution, and the weakness of the detective's story, he declared that they should prove, in behalf of the defendant, that he was not at or near the breaker until after the fire was well under way, and that the saving of a large portion of the company's loose property from destruction was due to his brave and energetic efforts.

"Furthermore," continued Pleadwell, earnestly, "we shall present to the court and jury a most irreproachable witness, who will testify to you that he was present and saw this fire kindled, and that the man who kindled it was *not* Jack Rennie."

[82]

There was a buzz of excitement in the court-room as Pleadwell resumed his seat; and Tom's heart beat loudly as he understood the significance of the lawyer's last statement. He felt, more than ever, the wrong, the disgrace, the self-humiliation to which he should stoop, by giving his testimony in support of so monstrous a lie.

But what could he do? The strain on his mind was terrible. He felt an almost irresistible desire to cry out, there, in the crowded court-room, that he had yielded to temptation for the sake of blind Bennie; that he had seen the folly and the wickedness, and known the awful misery of it already; that the money that bought him was like rags in his sight; and that his own guilt and cowardice should save this criminal no longer from the punishment which his crime deserved.

By a strong effort, he repressed his emotion, and sat, with face flushed and pallid by turns, waiting for the time when his wretched bargain should be fulfilled.

The first witness called on the part of[83] the defence was Michael Carolan, better known as "Silent Mike."

He testified that Rennie came down from Scranton with him and a body of strikers on the morning of November 18; that they ate supper with Carolan's married sister, who lived in the village, just beyond the burned breaker; that they spent the evening at a miners' mass-meeting in town, and afterwards called at a drinking-saloon; and that they were on the way back to his sister's house, for the night, when they heard the cry of "Fire!"

"At this time," continued Carolan, "Jack and me were together at the crossin' on Railroad Street, maybe a quarter of a mile away from the breaker, an' whin we heard the alarm, we looked up the track an' saw the blaze, an' Jack says, says he, 'Mike, the breaker's a-fire,' an' I says, says I, 'It is, sure;' an' with that we both ran up the track toward the fire.

"Whin we were most there we met Sandy McCulloch comin' from the hill beyant, an' me an' him an' Jack wint an' shoved out the cars from the loadin'-place[84] that we could get at; an' thin we wint to help with the furniture at the dwellin'-house, an' we saved ivery thing we could."

Silent Mike had done well. Few people had ever before heard so many words come in succession from his lips, and he told his story with such impressive earnestness that it was easy to believe that he spoke the truth. Indeed, there was very little in his account of the occurrence that was not strictly in accordance with the facts. He had simply omitted to state that he and Rennie had gone, first, up to the breaker and kindled the blaze, and then returned, hastily, to the crossing where they certainly were when the first cry of "Fire!" was heard.

Rennie's case was looking up. There was a recess for dinner, and, when court was re-opened, Sandy McCulloch was put on the witness-stand.

He was just getting into bed, he said, when he heard the cry of "Fire!" He looked out and saw that the breaker was burning, and, hurrying on his clothes, he ran down the hill.

[85]

"When I cam' to the fit o' the hill," he continued, in answer to Pleadwell's question, "I heard some'at behin' me, an' I lookit aroun', an' there I see Jack the Giant an' Silent Mike a-speedin' up the track toward the breaker.

"The fire was a-burnin' up brisk by then, an' me an' Jack an' Mike, we went an' pushit some cars out fra the loadin'-place, down the track; an' then we savit a bit fra the dwellin'-

18

house, an' a bit fra the engine-room, an' a bit here an' there, as we could; an' Jack, he workit like a' possessed, he did, sir; sure he did."

"What were you doing up so late at night?" was the first question put to Sandy on cross-examination.

"Well, you see, sir, a bit o' a lad that works i' the mines wi' us, he had lost his brither i' the slope the day, he had; an' I gied him a promise to help seek him oot gin he cam' i' the evenin' to say as the lad was no' foond; an' I was a-waitin' up for him, min' ye."

"Well, did the lad come?" inquired Lawyer Summons, somewhat sarcastically.

[86]

"He did that, an' he tellit me as how he'd foond the brither, an' leadit him hame, an' would na want me; an' I said 'good-nicht' till the lad, an' started to bed, an' the clock struckit eleven."

"Who was the lad that came to your house?"

"Tom Taylor, sir."

Rennie started in his seat as the name was spoken, and the blood mounted into his pale forehead as he gazed intently at the witness.

"Did the boy go in the direction of the breaker from your house?" questioned Summons.

"He did, sir."

"How long was it after he left you that you heard the cry of fire?"

"Well, maybe the time o' ten minutes."

"Could the boy have got beyond the breaker?"

"He must 'a', sir, he must 'a'; the grass was na growin' under his feet goin' doon the hill."

"Do you think Tom Taylor fired that breaker?"

[87]

Sandy stared for a moment in blank amazement.

"Why, the guid Lord bless ye, mon! be ye daft? There ain't a better boy i' the roun' warl'n Tom Taylor!" and Sandy broke into a hearty laugh at the very idea of Tom doing any thing wrong.

But Tom, who sat back in his seat and heard it all, was suddenly startled with the sense of a new danger. Suppose *he* should be charged with setting fire to the breaker? And suppose Rennie and Carolan should go upon the witness-stand and swear that they saw him running away from the newly kindled blaze, as, indeed, they might and not lie, either,—how could he prove his innocence? Yet he was about to swear Jack Rennie into freedom, knowing him to be guilty of the crime with which he was charged, and, what was still more despicable, he was about to do it for money.

Looked upon in this light, the thing that Tom had promised to do rose very black and ugly in his sight; and the poor delusion that he should tell no lie was swept, like a clinging cobweb, from his mind.

[88]

It was while his heart was still throbbing violently under the excitement of this last thought and fear, that he heard some one call,—

"Thomas Taylor!"

"Here, sir," responded Tom.

"Take the witness-stand."

[89]

CHAPTER V.
THE VERDICT.

Pale and trembling, Tom passed out into the aisle and down around the jury-box, and stepped upon the little railed platform.

In impressive tones, the clerk administered to him the oath, and he kissed the Holy Bible and swore to "tell the truth, the whole truth, and nothing but the truth."

The whole truth!

The words echoed and re-echoed through his mind, as he looked down upon the lawyers and jurors, and across the bar into the hundreds of expectant faces turned toward him. For a moment he felt frightened and dizzy.

But only for a moment; fear gave place to astonishment, for Jack Rennie had started to his feet, with wild eyes and face[90] blanched with sudden dread, and, bending over till his great beard swept Pleadwell's shoulder, he whispered, hoarsely, into the lawyer's ear, in a tone audible throughout the room,—

"Ye did na tell me who the lad was! He mus' na be sworn; it's na lawfu'. I'll no' have it; I say I'll no' have it!"

In another moment Pleadwell had his hand on the man's shoulder, and forced him into a seat. There was a whispered consultation of a few minutes between attorney and client, and then, while Rennie sat with his eyes turned steadfastly away from the witness, his huge hand clutching the edge of the table, and the expression of nervous dread still on his face, Pleadwell, calmly, as if there had been no interruption, proceeded with the examination.

He asked Tom about his residence and his occupation, and about how blind Bennie lost himself in the mines. With much skill, he carried the story forward to the time when Tom said good-night to Sandy, and started down the hill toward home.

[91]

"As you approached the breaker, did you see a man pass by you in the shadow?"

"I did," replied Tom.

"About how far from you?"

"I don't know; ten feet, maybe."

"Where did he go?"

"Around the corner, by the engine-room."

"From what point did he come?"

"From the loading-place."

"How long after he left the loading-place was it that you saw the first blaze there?"

"Two or three minutes, maybe."

"Did you see his face?"

"I did."

"How did he look? Describe him."

"He was short and thin, and had no whiskers."

Pleadwell pointed to Rennie, and asked,—

"Was this the man?"

"No, sir," answered Tom.

Pleadwell leaned back in his chair, and turned to the jury with a smile of triumph on his face. The people in the court-room nodded to each other, and whispered, "That clears Jack."

[92]

Every one, but Jack Rennie himself, seemed to feel the force of Tom's testimony. The prisoner still sat clutching the table, looking blankly at the wall, pale, almost trembling, with some suppressed emotion.

But through Tom's mind kept echoing the solemn words of his oath: "The whole truth; *the whole truth.*" And he had not told it; his testimony was no better than a lie. An awful sense of guilt came pressing in upon him from above, from below, from every side. Hateful voices seemed sounding in his brain: "Perjurer in spirit! Receiver of bribes!"

The torture of his self-abhorrence, in that one moment of silence, was terrible beyond belief.

Then a sudden impulse seized him; a bright, brave, desperate impulse.

He stepped down from the witness-stand, passed swiftly between chairs and tables, tearing the money from his breast-pocket by the way, and flinging the hated hundred dollars down before the astonished Pleadwell, he returned as quickly as he came,[93] stepped into his place with swelling breast and flaming cheeks and flashing eyes, and exclaimed, falling, in his excitement, into the broad accent of his mother tongue,—

"Noo I'm free! Do what ye wull wi' me! Prison me, kill me, but I'll no' hold back the truth longer for ony mon, nor a' the money that ony mon can gi' me!"

Men started to their feet in astonishment. Some one back among the people began to applaud. Jack Rennie turned his face toward the boy with a look of admiration, and his eyes were blurred with sudden tears.

"He's the son o' his father!" he exclaimed; "the son o' his father! He's a braw lad, an' good luck till him, but it was flyin' i' the face o' fortune to swear him. I told ye! I told ye!"

"Who gave you that money?" asked the district attorney of Tom, when quiet had been partially restored.

Pleadwell was on his feet in an instant.

"Stop!" he shouted. "Don't answer that question! Did I give you that money?"

[94]

"No, sir," replied Tom, awed by the man's vehemence.

"Did Jack Rennie give you that money?"

"No, sir."

Pleadwell turned to the court.

"Then if your Honors please, we object to the witness answering this question. This is a desperate theatrical trick, concocted by the prosecution to prejudice this defendant. We ask that they be not allowed to support it with illegal evidence."

The judge turned to Tom.

"Do you know," he asked, "that this money was given to you by the defendant's authority, or by his knowledge or consent?"

"I can't swear that it was," replied Tom.

"The objection is sustained," said his Honor, abruptly.

Pleadwell had gained a point; he might yet win the day. But the district attorney would not loose his grip.

"Why did you just give that money to the attorney for the defence?" he asked.

Pleadwell interposed another objection, but the court ruled that the question was properly in the line of cross-examination[95] of the defendant's witness, and Tom answered,—

"'Cause I had no right to it, an' he knows who it belongs to."

"Whom does it belong to?"

"I don't know, sir. I only know who gave it to me."

"When was it given to you?"

"A week ago last Thursday, sir."

"Where was it given to you?"

"In Mr. Pleadwell's office."

"Was Mr. Pleadwell present?"

"No, sir."

"How much money was given to you?"

"One hundred dollars, sir."

"For what purpose was it given to you?"

"To send my blind brother away to get his sight."

"I mean what were you to do in consideration of receiving the money?"

Before Tom could answer, Pleadwell was addressing the court:

"I submit, your Honor," he said, "that this inquisition has gone far enough. I protest against my client being prejudiced[96] by the unauthorized and irrelevant conduct of any one."

The judge turned to the district attorney. "Until you can more closely connect the defendant or his authorized agent," he said, "with the giving of this money, we shall be obliged to restrict you in this course of inquiry."

Pleadwell had made another point. He still felt that the case was not hopeless.

Then Summons, the private counsel for the prosecution, took the witness. "Tom," he said, "did you tell the truth in your direct examination?"

"I did, sir," replied Tom, "but not the whole truth."

"Well, then, suppose you tell the rest of it."

"I object," interposed Pleadwell, "to allowing this witness to ramble over the field of legal and illegal evidence at will. If counsel has questions to ask, let him ask them."

21

"We will see that the witness keeps within proper limits," said the judge; then, turning to Tom, "Go on, sir."

|97|

"Well, you see," said Tom, "it was all just as I told it; only when I got to the bottom o' the hill, an' see that man go by me in the dark, I was s'prised like, an' I stopped an' listened. An' then I heard a noise in under the loadin'-place, an' then that man," pointing his trembling forefinger to Rennie, "came out, a-kind o' talkin' to himself. An' he said that was the last job o' that kind he'd ever do; that they put it on him 'cause he hadn't anybody to feel bad over him if he should get catched at it.

"An' then I see a blaze start up right where he come from, an' it got bigger an' bigger. An' then he turned an' see me, an' he grabbed me by the shoulders, an' he said, 'Don't you speak nor whisper, or I'll take the life o' ye,' or somethin' like that; I can't quite remember, I was so scared. An' then he pushed me down the track, an' he said, 'Run as fast as ever you can, an' don't you dare to look back.'

"An' I run, an' I didn't look back till the fire was a-burnin' up awful; an' then I went with the rest to look at it; an' he|98| was there, an' a-workin' desperate to save things, an'— an'—an' that's all."

Tom stopped, literally panting for breath. The jurors were leaning forward in their seats to catch every word, and over among the crowded benches, where the friends of the prisoner were gathered, there was a confused hum of voices, from which, now and then, rose angry and threatening words.

Rennie sat gazing intently upon Tom, as though fascinated by the boy's presence, but on his face there was no sign of disappointment or anger; only the same look of admiration that had come there when Tom returned the money.

He clutched Pleadwell's sleeve, and said to him,—

"That settles it, mon; that settles it. The spirit o' the dead father's i' the lad, an' it's no use o' fightin' it. I'll plead guilty noo, an' end it, an' tak ma sentence an' stan' it. How long'll it be, think ye?"

"Twenty years in the Penitentiary," answered Pleadwell, sharply and shortly.

Rennie dropped back in his chair, as though the lawyer had struck him.

|99|

"Twenty years!" he repeated; "twenty years! That's a main lang time; I canna stan' that; I canna live through it. I'll no' plead guilty. Do what ye can for me."

But there was little that Pleadwell could do now. His worst fears had been realized. He knew it was running a desperate risk to place on the witness-stand a boy with a conscience like Tom's; but he knew, also, that if he could get Tom's story out in the shape he desired to, and keep back the objectionable parts, his client would go free; and he had great faith in the power of money to salve over a bruised conscience.

He had tried it and failed; and there was nothing to do now but make the best of it.

He resumed his calm demeanor, and turned to Tom with the question,—

"Did you ever tell to me the story you have just now told on the witness-stand, or any thing like it?"

"I never did," answered Tom.

"Did you ever communicate to me, in any way, your alleged knowledge of Jack Rennie's connection with this fire?"

|100|

"No, sir."

Pleadwell had established his own innocence, so far as Tom's story was concerned at least, and he dismissed the boy from the witness-stand with a wave of his hand which was highly expressive of virtuous indignation.

Tom resumed his seat by the side of Sandy, whose mouth and eyes were still wide open with surprise and admiration, and who exclaimed, as he gave the boy's hand a hearty grip,—

"Weel done, Tommy, ma lad! weel done! I'm proud o' ye! an' Bennie'n the mither'll be prouder yet o' ye!"

And then, for the first time since the beginning of his trouble, Tom put his face in his hands and wept. But he felt that a great load had been lifted from his conscience, and that now he could look any man in the eye.

There were two or three unimportant witnesses sworn in rebuttal and sur-rebuttal, and the evidence was closed.

Pleadwell rose to address the jury, feeling that it was a useless task so far as his[101] client was concerned, but feeling, also, that he must exert himself to the utmost in order to rebut a strong presumption of questionable conduct on his own part.

He denounced Tom's action in returning the money to him as a dramatic trick, gotten up by the prosecution for effect; and called particular attention to his own ignorance of the gift of any such money.

He declared Tom's story of his meeting with Rennie, on the night of the fire, to be improbable and false, and argued that since neither the prosecution, nor the defence, nor any one else, had ever heard one word of it till it came out on the witness-stand, it must, therefore, exist only in the lad's heated imagination.

He dwelt strongly on the probable falsity of the testimony of the so-called detective; went over carefully the evidence tending to establish an *alibi* for Rennie; spoke with enthusiasm of the man's efforts and bravery in the work of rescue; lashed the corporations for their indifference to the wrongs of the workingmen; spoke piteously of the fact that the[102] law denied to Rennie the right of being sworn in his own behalf; and closed with a peroration that brought tears into the eyes of half the people in the room.

He had made a powerful speech, and he knew it; but he thought of its effect only as tending to his own benefit; he had no hope for Rennie.

Mr. Summons addressed the jury on the part of the Commonwealth. He maintained that the evidence of the detective, taken in connection with all the other circumstances surrounding the case, was sufficient to have convicted the defendant, without further proof.

"But the unexpected testimony," he declared, "of one brave and high-minded boy has placed the guilt of the prisoner beyond the shadow of a doubt; a boy whose great heart has caused him to yield to temptation for the sake of a blind brother; but whose tender conscience, whose heroic spirit, has led him to throw off the bonds which this defence has placed upon him, and, in the face of all the terrors of an order whose words are oaths of vengeance, and whose[103] acts are deeds of blood, to fling their hated bribes at their feet, as they sat in the very court of justice; and to 'tell the truth, the whole truth, and nothing but the truth,' for the sake of his own honor and the upholding of the law."

Warming up to his theme, and its possibilities in the way of oratorical effect, Summons brought wit to bear upon logic and logic upon law, and eloquence upon both, until, at the close of his address, the conviction of the defendant was all but certain, and Tom's position as a hero was well assured.

Then came the charge of the court; plain, decisive, reviewing the evidence in brief, calling the attention of the jury to their duty both to the Commonwealth and to the defendant, directing them that the defendant's guilt must be established, in their minds, beyond a reasonable doubt, before they could convict; but that, if they should reach that point, then their verdict should be simply "Guilty."

The jury passed out of the court-room, headed by a constable, after which counsel[104] for the defendant filed exceptions to the charge, and the court proceeded to other business.

Very few people left the court-room, as every one supposed it would not be long before the bringing in of a verdict, and they were not mistaken. It was barely half an hour from the time the jury retired until they filed back again, and resumed their seats in the jury-box.

"Gentlemen of the jury," said the clerk of the court, rising, "have you agreed upon a verdict?"

"We have," replied the foreman, handing a paper to a tipstaff, which he handed to the clerk; and the clerk in turn handed it to the presiding judge.

The judges, one after another, read the paper, nodded their approval, and returned it to the clerk, who glanced over its contents, and then addressed the jury as follows:—

"Gentlemen of the jury, hearken unto your verdict as the court have it recorded. In the case wherein the Commonwealth is plaintiff and Jack Rennie is defendant, you[105] say you find the defendant *guilty*. So say you all?"

The members of the jury nodded their heads, the clerk resumed his seat, and the trial of Jack Rennie was concluded.

It was what every one had anticipated, and people began to leave the court-room, with much noise and confusion.

Rennie was talking, in a low tone, with Pleadwell and Carolan, while the sheriff, who had advanced to take charge of the prisoner, stood waiting for them to conclude the conference.

"I don't want the lad harmed," said Rennie, talking earnestly to Carolan, "him, nor his mither, nor his brither; not a hair o' his head, nor a mou'-ful o' his bread, noo min' ye—I ha' reasons—the mon that so much as lays a straw i' the lad's path shall suffer for't, if I have to live a hunder' year to tak' ma vengeance o' him!"

The sonorous voice of the court-crier, adjourning the courts until the following morning, echoed through the now half-emptied room, and the sheriff said to Rennie,—

[106]

"Well, Jack, I'm waiting for you."

"Then ye need na wait longer, for I'm ready to go wi' ye, an' I'm hungry too." And Rennie held out his hands to receive the handcuffs which the sheriff had taken from his pocket. For some reason, they would not clasp over the man's huge wrists.

"Oh!" exclaimed the officer, "I have the wrong pair. Simpson," turning to his deputy, "go down to my office and bring me the large handcuffs lying on my table."

Simpson started, but the sheriff called him back.

"Never mind," he said, "it won't pay; Jack won't try to get away from us, will you, Jack?" drawing a revolver from his pocket as he spoke, and grasping it firmly in his right hand, with his finger on the trigger.

"D'ye tak' me for a fool, mon?" said Rennie, laughing, as he glanced at the weapon; then, turning to Carolan and Pleadwell, he continued, "Good-nicht; good-nicht and sweet dreams till ye!" Jack had never seemed in a gayer mood[107] than as he marched off through the side-door, with the sheriff and his deputy; perhaps it was the gayety of despair.

Carolan had not replied to the prisoner's cheery "good-nicht." He had looked on at the action of the sheriff, with a curious expression in his eyes, until the trio started away, and then he had hurried from the court-room at a gait which made Pleadwell stare after him in astonishment.

It was dark outside; very dark. A heavy fog had come up from the river and enshrouded the entire city. The street-lamps shone but dimly through the thick mist, and a fine rain began to fall, as Tom and Sandy hurried along to their hotel, where they were to have supper, before going, on the late train, to their homes.

Up from the direction of the court-house came to their ears a confusion of noises; the shuffling of many feet, loud voices, hurried calls, two pistol-shots in quick succession; a huge, panting figure pushing by them, and disappearing in the fog and darkness; by and by, excited men hurrying toward them.

[108]

"What's the matter?" asked Sandy.

And some one, back in the mist, replied,—

"Jack Rennie has escaped!"

[109]

CHAPTER VI.
THE FALL.

It was true. Carolan's quick eye had noticed the opportunity for Rennie to escape, and his fertile brain had been swift in planning an immediate rescue. The few members of his order that he could find on the instant were gathered together; there was a sudden onslaught at a dark corner of the Court-House Square; the sheriff and his deputy lay prone upon the ground, and their prisoner was slipping away through the dark, foggy streets, with a policeman's bullet whizzing past his ears, and his band of rescuers struggling with the amazed officers.

But the sheriff of Luzerne County never saw Jack Rennie again, nor was the hand of the law ever again laid upon him, in arrest or punishment.

[110]

As Tom walked home from the railroad station that night through the drizzling rain, his heart was lighter than it had been for many a day.

True, he was nervous and worn with excitement and fatigue, but there was with him a sense of duty done, even though tardily, which brought peace into his mind and lightness to his footsteps.

After the first greetings were had, and the little home group of three was seated together by the fire to question and to talk, Tom opened his whole heart. While his mother and Bennie listened silently, often with tears, he told the story of his adventure at the breaker on the night of the fire, of his temptation and fall at Wilkesbarre, of his mental perplexity and acute suffering, of the dramatic incidents of the trial, and of his own release from the bondage of bribery.

When his tale was done, the poor blind brother, for whose sake he had stepped into the shadow of sin, and paid the penalty, declared, with laughter and with tears, that he had never before been so proud of Tom[111] and so fond of him as he was at that moment; and the dear, good mother took the big fellow on her lap, as she used to do when he was a little child, and held him up close to her heart, and rocked him till he fell asleep, and into his curly hair dropped now and then a tear, that was not the outcome of sorrow, but of deep maternal joy.

It was well along in December before the strike came to an end. There had been rumors for a week of an approaching compromise between the miners and the operators, but one day there came word that all hands were to be at the mines, ready for work, the following morning.

It was glad news for many a poor family, who saw the holidays approaching in company with bitter want; and it brought especial rejoicing to the little household dependent so largely on the labor of Tom and Bennie for subsistence.

The boys were at the entrance to the mine the next morning before the stars began to pale in the east. They climbed into a car of the first trip, and rode down the slope to the music of echoes roaring[112] through galleries that had long been silent.

The mules had been brought in the day before, and Tom ran whistling to the mine stables to untie his favorite Billy, and set him to his accustomed task. There came soon a half-dozen or more of driver-boys, and such a shouting and laughing and chattering ensued as made the beasts prick up their long ears in amazement.

"All aboard!" shouted Tom, as he fastened his trace-hook to the first trip of cars. "Through train to the West! No stops this side o' Chicorgo!"

"'Commodation ahead! Parly cars on the nex' train, an' no porters 'lowed!" squeaked out a little fellow, backing his mule up to the second trip.

"I'll poke the fire a bit an' git the steam up fur yez," said Patsy Donnelly, the most mischievous lad of them all. Whereupon he prodded Tom's mule viciously in the ribs, and that beast began playing such a tattoo with his heels against the front of the car as drowned all other noises in its clatter.

[113]

"Whoa, Billy!" shouted Tom, helping Bennie into the rear car of the trip. "Whoa, now! Stiddy—there, git-tup!" cracking his long leather whip-lash over Billy's ears as he spoke, and climbing into the front car. "Git-tup! Go it! Whoop!"

Away went Tom and Bennie, rattling up the long heading, imitating alternately the noise of the bell, the whistle, and the labored puffing of a locomotive engine; while the sound-waves, unable to escape from the narrow passage which confined them, rolled back into their ears in volumes of resounding echoes.

Ah, they were happy boys that morning! happy even though one was smitten with the desolation of blindness, and both were compelled to labor, from daylight to dark, in the grimy recesses of the mine, for the pittance that brought their daily bread; happy, because they were young and free-hearted and innocent, and contented with their lot.

And Tom was thrice happy, in that he had rolled away the burden of an accusing conscience, and felt the high pleasure that|114| nothing else on earth can so fully bring as the sense of duty done, against the frowning face and in the threatening teeth of danger.

Sometimes, indeed, there came upon him a sudden fear of the vengeance he might meet at Rennie's hands; but as the days passed by this fear disturbed him less and less, and the buoyancy of youth preserved him from depressing thoughts of danger.

Billy, too, was in good spirits that morning, and drew the cars rapidly along the heading, swinging around the sharp curves so swiftly that the yellow flame from the little tin lamp was blown down to the merest spark of blue; and stopping at last by the door in the entrance, where Bennie was to dismount and sit all day at his lonely task.

Three times Tom went down to the slope that morning, through Bennie's door, with his trip of loads, and three times he came back, with his trip of lights; and the third time he stopped to sit with his brother on the bench and to eat, from the one pail|115| which served them both, the plain but satisfying dinner which Mommie had prepared for them.

Tom was still light-hearted and jovial, but upon Bennie there seemed to have fallen since morning a shadow of soberness. To sit for hours with only one's thoughts for company, and with the oppressive silence broken only at long intervals by the passing trips, this alone is enough to cast gloom upon the spirits of the most cheerful.

But something more than this was weighing upon Bennie's mind, for he told Tom, when they had done eating, that every time it grew still around him, and there were no cars in the heading or airway, and no noises to break the silence, he could hear, somewhere down below him, the "working" of the mine. He had heard it all the morning he said, when every thing was quiet, and, being alone so, it made him nervous and afraid.

"I could stan' most any thing," he said, "but to get caught in a 'fall.'"

"Le's listen an' see if we can hear it now," said Tom.

|116|

Then both boys kept very quiet for a little while, and sure enough, over in the darkness, they heard an occasional snapping, like the breaking of dry twigs beneath the feet.

The process which the miners call "working" was going on. The pressure of the overlying mass of rock upon the pillars of coal left to support it was becoming so great that it could not be sustained, and the gradual yielding of the pillars to this enormous weight was being manifested by the crackling noises that proceeded from them, and the crumbling of tiny bits of coal from their bulging surfaces.

The sound of working pillars is familiar to frequenters of the mines, and is the well-known warning which precedes a fall. The remedy is to place wooden props beneath the roof for additional support, and, if this is not done, there comes a time, sooner or later, when the strained pillars suddenly give way, and the whole mass comes crashing down, to fill the gangways and chambers over an area as great as that through which the working extended,|117| and to block the progress of mining for an indefinite time.

Tom had been too long about the mines to be ignorant of all this, and so had Bennie; but they knew, too, that the working often continued weeks, and sometimes months, before the fall would take place, though it might, indeed, come at any moment.

That afternoon Tom told the slope boss about the working, and he came and made an examination, and said he thought there was no immediate danger, but that he would give orders to have the extra propping of the place begun on the following day.

"Jimmie Travis said he seen rats goin' out o' the slope, though, when he come in," said Tom, after relating to Bennie the opinion of the mine boss.

"Then 'twon't be long," replied Bennie, "'fore the fall comes."

He was simply echoing the belief of all miners, that rats will leave a mine in which a fall is about to take place. Sailors have the same belief concerning a ship about to sink.

|118|

"An' when the rats begin to go out," added Bennie, "it's time for men an' boys to think about goin' out too."

Somehow, the child seemed to have a premonition of disaster.

The afternoon wore on very slowly, and Bennie gave a long sigh of relief when he heard Tom's last trip come rumbling down the airway.

"Give me the dinner-pail, Bennie!" shouted Tom, as the door closed behind the last car, "an' you catch on behind—Whoa, Billy!" as the mule trotted on around the corner into the heading.

"Come, Bennie, quick! Give me your hand; we'll have to run to catch him now."

But even as the last word trembled on the boy's lips, there came a blast of air, like a mighty wind, and in the next instant a noise as of bursting thunder, and a crash that shook the foundations of the mines, and the two boys were hurled helplessly against Bennie's closed door behind them.

The fall had come.

The terrible roar died away in a series[119] of rumbling echoes, and, at last, stillness reigned.

"Bennie!"

It was Tom who spoke.

"Bennie!"

He called the name somewhat feebly.

"Bennie!"

It was a shout at last, and there was terror in his voice.

He raised himself to his feet, and stood leaning against the shattered frame-work of the door. He felt weak and dizzy. He was bruised and bleeding, too, but he did not know it; he was not thinking of himself, but of Bennie, who had not answered to his call, and who might be dead.

He was in total darkness, but he had matches in his pocket. He drew one out and stood, for a moment, in trembling hesitancy, dreading what its light might disclose. Then he struck it, and there, almost at his feet, lay his cap, with his lamp still attached to it.

He lighted the lamp and looked farther.

At the other side of the entrance, half-hidden by the wreck of the door, he saw[120] Bennie, lying on his side, quite still. He bent down and flashed the light into Bennie's face. As he did so the blind boy opened his eyelids, sighed, moved his hands, and tried to rise.

"Tom!"

The word came in a whisper from his lips.

"Yes, Bennie, I'm here; are you hurt?"

"No—yes—I don't know; what was it, Tom?"

"The fall, I guess. Can you get up? Here, I'll help you."

Bennie gained his feet. He was not much hurt. The door had given way readily when the boys were forced against it, and so had broken the severity of the shock. But both lads had met with some cuts and some severe bruises.

"Have you got a lamp, Tom?"

"Yes; I just found it; come on, let's go home."

Tom took Bennie's hand and turned to go out, but the first step around the pillar, into the heading, brought him face to face with a wall of solid rock which filled every[121] inch of the passage. It had dropped, like a curtain, blotting out, in one instant, the mule and the cars, and forming an impassable barrier to the further progress of the boys in that direction.

"We can't get out this way," said Tom; "we'll have to go up through the airway."

They went back into the airway, and were met by a similar impenetrable mass.

Then they went up into the short chambers beyond the airway, and Tom flashed the light of his lamp into every entrance, only to find it blocked and barred by the roof-rock from the fall.

"We'll have to go back up the headin'," said Tom, at last, "an' down through the old chambers, an' out to the slope that way."

But his voice was weak and cheerless, for the fear of a terrible possibility had grown up in his mind. He knew that, if the fall extended across the old chambers to the west wall of the mine, as was more than likely, they were shut in beyond hope of escape, perhaps beyond

27

hope of rescue; and if such were to be their fate, then it|122| would have been far better if they were lying dead under the fallen rock, with Billy and the cars.

Hand in hand the two boys went up the heading, to the first opening in the lower wall, and creeping over the pile of "gob" that partially blocked the entrance, they passed down into a series of chambers that had been worked out years before, from a heading driven on a lower level.

Striking across through the entrances, in the direction of the slope, they came, at last, as Tom had expected and feared, to the line of the fall: a mass of crushed coal and broken rock stretching diagonally across the range of chambers towards the heading below.

But perhaps it did not reach to that heading; perhaps the heading itself was still free from obstruction!

This was the only hope now left; and Tom grasped Bennie's hand more tightly in his, and hurried, almost ran, down the long, wide chamber, across the airway and into the heading.

They had gone scarce twenty rods along|123| the heading, when that cruel, jagged wall of rock rose up before them, marking the confines of the most cheerless prison that ever held a hopeless human being.

When Tom saw it he stopped, and Bennie said, "Have we come to it, Tom?"

Tom answered: "It's there, Bennie," and sank down upon a jutting rock, with a sudden weakness upon him, and drew the blind boy to a seat beside him.

"We're shut in, Bennie," he said. "We'll never get out till they break a way into us, and, maybe, by the time they do that, it'll be—'twon't be worth while."

Bennie clung tremblingly to Tom; but, even in his fright, it came into his mind to say something reassuring, and, thinking of his lonesome adventure on the day of the strike, he whispered, "Well, 'taint so bad as it might be, Tom; they might 'a' been one of us shut up here alone, an' that'd 'a' been awful."

"I wish it had 'a' been one of us alone," answered Tom, "for Mommie's sake. I wish it'd 'a' been only me. Mommie|124| couldn't ever stan' it to lose—both of us—like—this."

For their own misfortune, these boys had not shed a tear; but, at the mention of Mommie's name, they both began to weep, and, for many minutes, the noise of their sobbing and crying was the only sound heard in the desolate heading.

Tom was the first to recover.

A sense of the responsibility of the situation had come to him. He knew that strength was wasted in tears. And he knew that the greater the effort towards physical endurance, towards courage and manhood, the greater the hope that they might live until a rescuing party could reach them. Besides this, it was his place, as the older and stronger of the two, to be very brave and cheerful for Bennie's sake. So he dried his tears, and fought back his terror, and spoke soothing words to Bennie, and even as he did so, his own heart grew stronger, and he felt better able to endure until the end, whatever the end might be.

"God can see us, down in the mine, just|125| as well as He could up there in the sunlight," he said to Bennie, "an' whatever He'd do for us up there He'll do for us down here. An' there's them 'at won't let us die here, either, w'ile they've got hands to dig us out; an' I shouldn't wonder—I shouldn't wonder a bit—if they were a-diggin' for us now."

After a time, Tom concluded that he would pass up along the line of the fall, through the old chambers, and see if there was not some opening left through which escape would be possible.

So he took Bennie's hand again, and led him slowly up through the abandoned workings, in and out, to the face of the fall at every point where it was exposed, only to find, always, the masses of broken and tumbled rock, reaching from floor to roof.

Yet not always! Once, as Tom flashed the lamp-light up into a blocked entrance, he discovered a narrow space between the top of the fallen rock and the roof, and, releasing Bennie's hand, and climbing up to it, with much difficulty, he found that he|126| was able to crawl through into a little open place in the next chamber.

From here he passed readily through an unblocked entrance into the second chamber, and, at some little distance down it, he found another open entrance. The light of hope flamed up in his breast as he crept along over the smooth, sloping surfaces of fallen rock, across one chamber after another, nearer and nearer to the slope, nearer and nearer to freedom, and the blessed certainty of life. Then, suddenly, in the midst of his reviving hope, he came to a place where the closest scrutiny failed to reveal an opening large enough for even his small body to force its way through. Sick at heart, in spite of his self-determined courage, he crawled back through the fall, up the free passages and across the slippery rocks, to where Bennie stood waiting.

"I didn't find any thing," he said, in as strong a voice as he could command. "Come, le's go on up."

He took Bennie's hand and moved on. But, as he turned through an entrance into the next chamber, he was startled to see,[127] in the distance, the light of another lamp. The sharp ears of the blind boy caught the sound of footsteps.

"Somebody's comin', Tom," he said.

"I see the lamp," Tom answered, "but I don't know who it can be. There wasn't anybody in the new chambers w'en I started down with the load. All the men went out quite a bit ahead o' me."

The two boys stood still; the strange light approached, and, with the light, appeared, to Tom's astonished eyes, the huge form and bearded face of Jack Rennie.

[128]
CHAPTER VII.
THE SHADOW OF DEATH.

"Why, lads!" exclaimed Rennie; "lads!" Then, flashing the light of his lamp into the boys' faces, "What, Tom, is it you? you and the blind brither? Ah! but it's main bad for ye, bairnies, main bad—an' warse yet for the poor mither at hame."

When Tom first recognized Rennie, he could not speak for fear and amazement. The sudden thought that he and Bennie were alone, in the power of this giant whose liberty he had sworn away, overcame his courage. But when the kindly voice and sympathizing words fell on his ears, his fear departed, and he was ready to fraternize with the convict, as a companion in distress.

"Tom," whispered Bennie, "I know his[129] voice. It's the man 'at talked so kind to me on the day o' the strike."

"I remember ye, laddie," said Jack. "I remember ye richt well." Then, turning to Tom, "Ye were comin' up the fall; did ye find any openin'?"

"No," said Tom, speaking for the first time since the meeting; "none that's any good."

"An' there's naught above, either," replied Jack; "so we've little to do but wait. Sit ye doon, lads, an' tell me how ye got caught."

Seated on a shelf of rock, Tom told in a few words how he and Bennie had been shut in by the fall. Then Jack related to the boys the story of his escape from the sheriff, and how his comrades had spirited him away into these abandoned workings, and were supplying him with food until such time as he could safely go out in disguise, and take ship for Europe.

There he was when the crash came.

"Noo ye mus' wait wi' patience," he said. "It'll no' be for lang; they'll soon be a-comin' for ye. The miners ha' strong[130] arms an' stoot herts, an' ye'll hear their picks a-tap-tappin' awa' i' the headin'—to-morrow, mayhap."

"An' is it night now?" asked Bennie.

"It mus' be, lad. I ha' naught to mark the time by, but it mus' be along i' the evenin'."

"But," interrupted Tom, as the thought struck him, "if they find you here, you'll have to go back to the jail."

"I ha' thocht o' that," answered Jack. "I ha' thocht o' that, an' my min's made up. I'll go back, an' stan' ma sentence. I ha' deserved it. I'd ha' no peace o' min' a-wanderin' o'er the earth a-keepin' oot o' the way o' the law. An' maybe, if I lived ma sentence oot, I could do some'at that's better. But I'll no' hide any longer; I canna do it!"

Off somewhere in the fall there was a grinding, crunching sound for a minute, and then a muffled crash. Some loosened portion of the roof had fallen in.

For a long time Jack engaged the boys in conversation, holding their minds as much as possible from the fate of imprisonment.

[131]

Toward midnight Bennie complained of feeling hungry, and Jack went down into the old chambers where he had been staying, and came back after a while with a basket of food and a couple of coarse blankets, and then they all went up to Bennie's doorway. Tom's oil was up there, and their lamps needed filling. It seemed more like home up there too; and, besides that, it was the point toward which a rescuing party would be most likely to work.

Jack's basket was only partly full of food, but there would be enough, he thought, to last, by economical use, during the following day. He ate none of it himself, however, and the boys ate but sparingly.

Then they made up a little platform from the boards and timbers of the ruined door, and spread the blankets on it, and induced Bennie, who seemed to be weak and nervous, to lie down on it and try to sleep. But the lad was very restless, and slept only at intervals, as, indeed, did Tom and Jack, one of whom had stretched himself out on the bench, while the other[132] sat on the mine floor, reclining against a pillar.

When they thought it was morning, they all arose and walked around a little, and the boys ate another portion of the food from the basket. But Jack did not touch it; he was not hungry, he said, and he went off into the new chambers to explore the place.

After a while he came back and sat down, and began telling stories of his boyhood life in the old country, intermingling with them many a marvellous tale and strange adventure, and so he entertained the boys for hours.

It must have been well on into the afternoon that Tom took to walking up and down the heading. Sometimes Jack went with him, but oftener he remained to talk with Bennie, who still seemed weak and ill, and who lay down on the blankets again later on, and fell asleep.

The flame of the little lamp burned up dimly. More oil and a fresh wick were put in, but the blaze was still spiritless.

Jack knew well enough what the trouble[133] was. There were places up in the new chambers where the deadly carbonic acid gas was escaping into the prison, adding, with terrible rapidity, to the amount produced by exhalation and combustion. But he said nothing; the boys did not know, and it would be useless to alarm them further.

Bennie started and moaned now and then in his sleep, and finally awoke, crying. He had had bad dreams, he said.

Jack thought it must be late in the second evening of their imprisonment.

He took all the food from the basket, and divided it into three equal parts. It[134] would be better to eat it, he thought, before actual suffering from hunger began. They would be better able to hold out in the end.

Nevertheless, he laid his portion back in the basket.

"I haven't the stomach for it just noo," he said. "Mayhap it'll taste better an' I wait a bit."

There was plenty of water. A little stream ran down through the airway, from which the pail had been repeatedly filled.

The night wore on.

The first sound of rescue had not yet been heard.

By-and-by both boys slept.

Jack alone remained awake and thoughtful. His face gave token of great physical suffering. Once he lifted the cover from the basket, and looked hungrily and longingly at the little portion of food that remained. Then he replaced the lid, and set the basket back resolutely on the ledge.

"No! no!" he murmured. "I mus' na tak' it oot o' the mou's o' Tom Taylor's bairns."

[135]

For a long time he sat motionless, with his chin in his hands, and his eyes fixed on the sleeping lads. Then, straightening up, there came into his face a look of heroic resolution.

"I'll do it!" he said, aloud. "It'll be better for us a'."

The sound of his voice awakened Tom, who had slept for some hours, and who now arose and began again his monotonous walk up and down the heading.

After a while, Jack motioned to him to come and sit beside him on the bench.

"I ha' summat to say to ye," he said. Then, with a glance at the sleeping boy, "Come ye up the airway a bit."

The two walked up the airway a short distance, and sat down on a broken prop by the side of the track.

"Tom," said Jack, after a moment or two of silence, "it's a-goin' hard wi' us. Mos' like it's near two days sin' the fall, an' no soun' o' help yet. Na doot but they're a-workin', but it'll tak' lang to get here fra the time ye hear the first tappin'. The three o' us can't live that lang; mayhap[136] two can. Ye s'all be the ones. I ha' fixed on that fra the start. That's why I ha' ta'en no food."

"An' we've had it all!" broke in Tom. "You shouldn't a-done it. The three of us ought to a' fared alike—'cept, maybe, Bennie; he aint so strong, an' he ought to be favored."

"Yes, Tom, the weakes' first. That's richt; that's why I'm a-givin' my chances to you lads. An' besides that, my life ain't worth savin' any way, alongside o' yours an' Bennie's. Ye s'all share what's i' the basket atween ye. 'Tain't much, but it'll keep ye up as lang's the air'll support ye. It's a-gettin' bad, the air is. D'ye min' the lomp, how dim an' lazy-like it burns? A mon's got to ha' such strength as food'll give him to hold out lang in air like this."

"I wish you'd 'a' eaten with us," interrupted Tom again. "'Tain't right to let your chances go that way on account of us."

Paying no attention to this protest, Jack continued:

"But I've a thing on ma min', Tom, that[137] I'd feel easier aboot an' fitter for what's a-comin' if I told it. It's aboot the father, lad; it's aboot Tom Taylor, an' how he cam' to his death. Ye'll no' think too hard o' me, Tom? It wasna the fall o' top coal that killit him—it was me! Tom! lad! Tom! bear wi' me a minute! Sit ye an' bear wi' me; it'll no' be for lang."

The boy had risen to his feet, and stood staring at the man in terrified amazement. Then Jack rose, in his turn, and hurried on with his story:

"It wasna by intent, Tom. We were the best o' frien's; I was his butty. We had a chamber thegither that time i' the Carbondale mine. But one day we quarrelled,—I've no call to say what aboot,—we quarrelled there in the chamber, an' ugly words passed, an' there cam' a moment when one o' us struck the ither.

"Then the fight began; han' to han'; both lamps oot; a' in the dark; oh, it was tarrible! tarrible!—doon on the floor o' the mine, crashin' up against the ragged pillars, strugglin' an' strainin' like mad—an' a' of a sudden, I heard a sharp cry, an' I[138] felt him a-slippin' oot o' ma arms an' doon to ma feet, an' he lay there an' was still.

"I foun' ma lamp an' lighted it, an' when I lookit at him, he was dead.

"I was a coward. I was afraid to say we'd been a-fightin'; I was afraid they'd say I murdered him. So I blastit doon a bit o' roof, an' fixed it like the top coal'd killit him; an' I wasna suspeckit. But I could na stay there; an' I wandered west, an' I wandered east, an' I took to drink, an' to evil deeds, an' at last I cam' back, an' I went in wi' the Molly Maguires—Scotchman as I was—an' I done desperate work for 'em; work that I oughtn't to be alive to-night to speak aboot—but I ha' suffered; O lad, I ha' suffered!

"Mony an' mony's the nicht, as often as I ha' slept an' dreamed, that I ha' fought over that fight i' the dark, an' felt that body a-slip, slippin' oot o' ma grasp. Oh, it's been tarrible, tarrible!"

Jack dropped into his seat again and buried his face in his hands.

The man's apparent mental agony melted[139] Tom's heart, and he sat down beside him and laid a comforting hand on his knee.

"I have naught against you," he said, and repeated, "I have naught against you."

After a while Jack looked up.

"I believe ye, lad," he said, "an' somehow I feel easier for the tellin'. But ye mus' na tell the mither aboot it, Tom; I've a reason for that. I've a bit o' money here, that I've saved along through the years, an' I've neither kith nor kin that's near enow to leave it wi'—an' I want she should have it; an' if she knew she might not tak' it."

As he spoke he drew, from an inner pocket, a folded and wrapped package, and gave it to Tom.

"It's a matter o' a thousan' dollars," he continued, "an' I'd like—I'd like if a part o' it could be used for gettin' sight for the blin' lad, gin he lives to get oot. I told him, one day, that he should have his sight, if money'd buy it—an' I want to keep ma ward."

Tom took the package, too much amazed, and too deeply moved to speak.

[140]

The grinding noise of settling rock came up from the region of the fall, and then, for many minutes, the silence was unbroken.

After a while, Jack said, "Put the money where they'll find it on ye, gin ye—gin ye don't get oot."

Then he rose to his feet again.

"You're not goin' to leave us?" said Tom.

"Yes, lad, I mus' go. It's the way wi' hunger, sometimes, to mak' a man crazy till he's not knowin' what he does. Ye s'all no ha' that to fear fra me. Tom," grasping the boy, suddenly, by both hands, "don't come up into the new chambers, Tom; promise me!"

Tom promised, and Jack added, "Mayhap I s'all not see ye again—good-by—keep up heart; that's the gret thing for both o' ye—keep up heart, an' never let hope go."

Then he loosed the boy's hands, picked up his lamp, and, with a smile on his face, he turned away. He passed down the airway, and out by the entrance where blind Bennie lay, still sleeping, and stopped[141] and looked tenderly down upon him, as men look, for the last time in life, on those whom they love.

He bent over, holding his heavy beard back against his breast, and touched the tangled hair on the child's forehead with his lips; and then, weak, staggering, with the shadow of his fate upon him, he passed out on the heading, and up into the new chambers, where the poisoned air was heavy with the deadly gas, and the lamp-flame scarcely left the wick; and neither Tom Taylor nor his blind brother ever saw Jack Rennie again, in life or in death.

When Tom went back to the waiting-place, Bennie awoke.

"I had such a nice dream, Tom," he said. "I thought I was a-lyin' in the little bed, at home, in the early mornin'; an' it was summer, an' I could hear the birds a-singin' in the poplar tree outside; an' then Mommie she come up by the bed an' kissed me; an' then I thought, all of a sudden, I could see. O Tom, it was lovely! I could see Mommie a-stannin' there, an' I could see the sunlight a-comin'[142] in at the window, an' a-shinin' on the floor; an' I jumped up an' looked out, an' it was all just like—just like heaven."

There was a pause, and then Bennie added, "Tom, do you s'pose if I should die now an' go to heaven, I could see up there?"

"I guess so," answered Tom; "but you aint goin' to die; we're goin' to get out—both of us."

But Bennie was still thinking of the heavenly vision.

"Then I wouldn't care, Tom; I'd just as lieve die—if only Mommie could be with me."

Again Tom spoke, in earnest, cheerful tones, of the probability of rescue; and discussed the subject long, and stimulated his own heart, as well as Bennie's, with renewed hope.

By-and-by the imperious demands of hunger compelled a resort to the remnant of food. Tom explained that Jack had gone away, to be by himself a while, and wanted them to eat what there was in the basket. Bennie did not question the[143] statement. So the last of the food was eaten.

After this there was a long period of quiet waiting, and listening for sounds of rescue, and, finally, both boys lay down again and slept.

Hours passed by with no sound save the labored breathing of the sleepers. Then Tom awoke, with a prickling sensation over his entire body, and a strange heaviness of the head and weakness of the limbs; but Bennie slept on.

"He might as well sleep," said Tom, to himself, "it'll make the time shorter for him."

But by and by Bennie awoke, and said that he felt very sick, and that his head was hurting him.

He fell asleep again soon, however, and it was not until some hours later that he awoke, with a start, and asked for water. After that, though oppressed with drowsiness, he slept only at intervals, and complained constantly of his head.

Tom cared for him and comforted him, putting his own sufferings out of sight;[144] sleeping a little, straining his ears for a sound of rescue.

The hours crept on, and the flame of the little lamp burned round and dim, and the deadly gas grew thicker in the darkness.

Once, after a longer period of quiet than usual, there came a whisper from Bennie.

"Tom!"

"What is it, Bennie?"

"Where did Jack go?"

"Up in the new chambers."

"How long's he been gone?"

"Oh, a day or two, I guess."

"Hark, Tom, is that him?"

"I don't hear any thing, Bennie."

"Listen! it's a kind o' tappin,' tappin'—don't you hear it?"

But Tom's heart was beating so wildly that he could hear no lesser noise.

"I don't hear it any more," said Bennie.

But both boys lay awake now and listened; and by and by Bennie spoke again, "There it is; don't you hear it, Tom?"

This time Tom did hear it; just the[145] faintest tap, tap, sounding, almost, as though it were miles away.

There was a little crowbar there, that had been brought down from the new chambers. Tom caught it up, and hurried into the heading, and beat, half a dozen times, on the wall there, and then, dropping the bar from sheer exhaustion, he lay down beside it and listened.

It was hard to tell if they heard his strokes, though he repeated them again and again, as his strength would permit.

But the faint tapping ceased only at intervals, and, once in a long while, a scarcely perceptible thud could be heard.

Tom crept back to Bennie, and tried to speak cheeringly, as they lay and listened.

But the blind boy's limbs had grown numb, and his head very heavy and painful. His utterance, too, had become thick and uncertain, and at times he seemed to be wandering in his mind. Once he started up, crying out that the roof was falling on him.

Hours passed. Echoing through the fall, the sound of pick and crowbar came, with unmistakable earnestness.

[146]

Tom had tapped many times on the wall, and was sure he had been heard, for the answering raps had reached his ears distinctly.

But they were so long coming; so long! Yet Tom nursed his hope, and fought off the drowsiness that oppressed him, and tried to care for Bennie.

The blind boy had got beyond caring for himself. He no longer heard the sounds of rescue. Once he turned partly on his side.

"Yes, Mommie," he whispered, "yes, I see it; ain't it pretty!" Then, after a pause, "O Mommie, how beautiful—how beautiful—it is—to see!"

Tap, tap, thud, came the sounds of rescue through the rock and coal.

Tap, tap, thud; but, oh, how the moments lagged; how the deadly gas increased; how the sharp teeth of hunger gnawed; how feebly burned the flame of the little lamp; how narrow grew the issue between life and death!

A time had come when Bennie could be no longer roused to consciousness, when[147] the brain itself had grown torpid, and the tongue refused to act.

Tap! tap! louder and louder; they were coming near, men's voices could be heard; thud! thud! the prison-wall began to tremble with the heavy blows; but the hours went slipping by into the darkness, and, over the rude couch, whereon the blind boy lay, the angel of death hung motionless, with pinions poised for flight.

"O God!" prayed Tom; "O dear God, let Bennie live until they come!"

|148|

CHAPTER VIII.
OUT OF DARKNESS.

It was with a light heart that the Widow Taylor kissed her two boys good-by that morning in December, and watched them as they disappeared into the fading darkness. When they were gone she went about her household duties with a song on her lips. She did not often sing when she was alone; but this was such a pretty little song of a mother and her boy, that on this happy winter morning she could not choose but sing it.

Hers were such noble boys, such bright, brave boys! They had given her heart and life to begin the struggle for bread, on that awful day when she found herself homeless, moneyless, among strangers in a strange land; when, in answer to her eager question for her husband, she had|149| been told that he had met an untimely death, and was already lying in his grave.

But, as she had toiled and trusted, her sons had grown, both in stature and in grace, till they had become, indeed, her crown of rejoicing.

One thing yet she looked forward to with eager hope, and that was the time when her blind boy might have the benefit of skilful treatment for his eyes, with the possibility of sight. It might take years of saving yet, but every day that they could all work made the time of waiting one day less. So she was hardly less rejoiced at the renewal of their tasks than were the boys themselves.

It was a bright day, and warm, too, for December; she thought of it afterward, how fair the day was. But it was lonely without her boys. It had been weeks since they had been away from her all day so; and, long before the sun went down, she began to wish for their coming.

She made supper early, and set out a few treasured dainties on the table, in honor of the first day's work. Then, while|150| the shadows grew indistinct, and the darkness settled down upon the earth, she sat by the window and saw the stars come out, and waited for her boys.

Suddenly there came a jar, the house rocked slightly, the windows rattled, and a dish on the pantry-shelf fell to the floor and was broken.

The Widow Taylor started to her feet, and stood, for a moment, wondering what it could mean. Then she opened the door of her cottage and looked out.

Other women were standing by their gates, and men were hurrying past her in the darkness.

"What's happened?" she called out, to a neighbor.

"A fall," came back the answer; "it must 'a' been a fall."

"Where?"

She asked the question with a dreadful apprehension settling down upon her.

"We canna tell; but mos' like it's i' the Dryden Slope. They're a-runnin' that way."

The widow shrank back into her house,|151| and sank, weakly, into a chair. For the moment she was overcome; but only for the moment. Hope came to her rescue. There were a hundred chances to one that her boys were not in the mine, even if the fall had been there; indeed, it was already time for them to be at home.

She waited, for a few moments, in anxious indecision; then, throwing a shawl about her head and shoulders, she went out into the night.

She knew very well the route by which her boys came from their work, and she determined to go until she should meet them. There were many people hurrying toward the slope, but only one man coming from it, and he was running for a doctor, and had no time to talk.

Increasing anxiety hastened the widow's steps. She could not go fast enough. Even as it was, people jostled by her in the darkness, and she ran to keep up with them.

34

At last, the mile that lay between her cottage and the mine was almost covered. Up on the hillside, at the mouth of the[152] slope, she saw the twinkling and glancing of the lights of many lamps. The crowds had grown more dense. Other women were pushing past her, moaning and lamenting.

She climbed the hill, and through the throng, to where a heavy rope had been stretched about the mouth of the slope, as a barrier to hold back the pressing crowd; and clutching the rope with both hands, she stood there and waited and watched.

She was where she could see into the opening of the mine, and where she could see all who came out.

Some cars were lowered from the slope-house to the mouth, and a dozen men, with picks and crowbars, climbed into them and went speeding down into the blackness. It was another rescuing party.

Across the open space before her, the widow saw Sandy McCulloch coming, and cried out to him, "Sandy!"

He stopped for an instant, then, recognizing the woman's voice, he came up to her, and laid his hands on hers, and, before she could speak again, he said, "Ye're lookin' for the lads. They're no' come oot yet."

[153]

"Sandy—are they safe?"

"We canna tell. There was mony 'at got this side o' the fall afoor it comed; an' some 'at got catched in it; an' mos' like there be some 'at's beyon' it."

A car came up the slope, and the body of a man was lifted out, placed on a rude stretcher, and carried by.

Sandy moved, awkwardly, to get between the dread sight and the woman's eyes. But she looked at it only for a moment. It was a man; and those she sought were not men, but boys.

"They're a-workin'," continued Sandy, "they're a-workin' like tigers to get to 'em, an' we're a-hopin'; that's a' we can do—work an' hope."

The man hurried away and left her, still standing there, to watch the car that came up from the blackness, at lengthening intervals, with its dreadful load, and to hear the shrill cry from some heart-broken wife and mother, as she recognized the victim. But they were always men who were brought out, not boys.

After a time, a party of workers came[154] up, exhausted, and others went down in their places. The men were surrounded with eager questioners, but they had little to say. The work of rescue was progressing, that was all.

By and by Sandy came back.

"Ye should no stay here, Mistress Taylor," he said. "When the lads be found ye s'all know it; I'll bring 'em to ye mysel'. Mos' like they're back o' the fall, an' it'll tak' time to get 'em—all nicht maybe, maybe longer; but when they're found, ye s'all not be long knowin' it."

"O Sandy! ye'll spare naught; ye'll spare naught for 'em?"

"We'll spare naught," he said.

He had started with her towards home, helping her along until the bend in the road disclosed the light in her cottage window; and then, bidding her to be hopeful, and of strong heart, he left her, and hurried back to aid in the work of rescue.

The outer line of the fall, and the openings into it, had already been searched; and all the missing had been accounted for—some living, some dead, and some to[155] whom death would have been a happy relief—all the missing, save Tom Taylor and his blind brother.

It was well known that their route to the foot of the slope lay by the new north heading; and, along this passage, the entire work of rescue was now concentrated. The boys would be found, either buried under the fall, or imprisoned back of it.

At some points in the heading, the rescuing parties found the rock and coal wedged in so solidly that the opening of a few feet was the work of an hour; again, the huge blocks and slabs were piled up, irregularly; and, again, there would be short distances that were wholly clear.

But no matter what these miners met, their work never for one moment ceased nor lagged. They said little; men do not talk much under a pressure like that; but every muscle was tense, every sense on the alert; they were at the supreme height of physical effort.

Such labor was possible only for a few hours at a time, but the tools scarcely ceased in their motion, so quickly were|156| they caught up by fresh hands, from the exhausted ones that dropped them.

Men do not work like that for money. No riches of earth could charge nerve and muscle with such energetic fire. It was, indeed, a labor of love.

There was not a workman in Dryden Slope but would have worn his fingers to the bone to save these lads, or their widowed mother, from one hour of suffering. The frank, manly character of Tom, and the pathetic simplicity of his blind brother, had made both boys the favorites of the mine. And beneath the grimy clothes of these rugged miners, beat hearts as warm and resolute as ever moved the noblest of earth's heroes to generous deeds of daring.

When the Widow Taylor reached home it was almost midnight. She set away the supper-dishes from the table, and, in place of them, she put some of her simple household remedies. She prepared bandages and lint, and made every thing ready for the restoration and comfort of the sufferers when they should arrive.

She expected that they would be weak,|157| wounded, too, perhaps; but she had not yet thought of them as dead.

Then she lay down upon her bed and tried to sleep; but at every noise she wakened; at every passing foot-fall she started to her feet.

At daybreak a miner stopped, with blackened face and bleeding hands, to tell her that the work of rescue was going bravely on. He had, himself, just come from the face of the new opening, he said; and would go back again, to work, after he had taken a little food and a little sleep.

The morning went by; noon passed, and still no other tidings. The monotony of waiting became unbearable at last, and the stricken woman started on another journey to the mine.

When she came near to the mouth of the slope, they made way for her in silent sympathy. A trip of cars came out soon after her arrival, and a half-dozen miners lifted themselves wearily to the ground. The crowd pressed forward with eager questions, but the tired workers only shook their heads. They feared, they said, that|158| not half the distance through the fall had yet been accomplished.

But one of them, a brawny, great-hearted Irishman, came over to where the Widow Taylor stood, white-faced and eager-eyed, and said, "It won't be long now, ma'am, till we'll be afther rachin' 'em. We're a-hopin' every blissed hour to break through to where the purty lads is a-sthayin'."

She started to ask some question, but he interrupted her:

"Oh, av coorse! av coorse! It's alive they are, sure; an' hearty; a bit hungry like, maybe, an' no wondher; but safe, ma'am, as safe as av ye had the both o' thim in your own house, an' the dure locked behind yez."

"An' do ye find no signs?" she asked. "Do ye hear no sounds?"

"Ah, now!" evading the question; "niver ye fear. Ye'll see both childer a-laughin' in your face or ever the mornin' dawns again, or Larry Flannigan's word's no betther than a lie."

She turned away and went home again, and the long night passed, and the morning|159| dawned, and Larry Flannigan's word was, indeed, no better than a lie.

It was only the same old story: "They're a-workin'. It can't be long now."

But among themselves the miners said that had the lads escaped the fall, they would perish from hunger and foul air long before the way could be opened into their prison. To bring their lifeless bodies out for decent burial was all that could be hoped.

The morning of the fourth day dawned, beautiful and sunny. It was the holy Christmas Day; the day on which the star-led shepherds found the Christ-child in the hallowed manger in the town of Bethlehem. White and pure upon the earth, in the winter sunlight, rested a covering of newly fallen snow; and, pale-faced and hollow-eyed, the mother of the two imprisoned boys looked out upon it from the window of her desolated home.

The sympathizing neighbors who had kept her company for the night had gone for a little while, and she was alone.

She knew that there was no hope.

[160]

They had thought it a kindness to tell her so at last, and she had thanked them for not keeping the bitter truth hid from her.

She did not ask any more that she might see her two boys in life; she only prayed now that their dear bodies might be brought to her unmangled, to be robed for Christian burial.

To this end she began now to make all things ready. She put in order the little best room; she laid out the clean, new clothing, and the spotless sheets; she even took from her worn purse the four small coins to place upon the white, closed lids.

In the locked cupboard, where the boys should not see them till the time came, she found the Christmas presents she had thought to give to them this day.

Not much, indeed. A few cheap toys, some sweetmeats purchased secretly, a book or two, and, last of all, some little gifts that her own weary, loving hands had wrought in the long hours after the children were asleep.

And now the Christmas dawn had come; but the children—

[161]

She had not wept before, not since the first jar from the fall had rocked her cottage; but now, with the sight of these poor, simple Christmas gifts, there came some softening influence that moved her heart, and brought the swift tears to her eyes, and she sat down in her accustomed chair and wept—wept long and piteously, indeed, but in the weeping found relief.

She was aroused by a knock at the door. The latch was lifted, the door pushed open, and Sandy McCulloch stumbled in. He was out of breath, his eyes were wide with excitement, and down each side of his grimy face was a furrow where the tears had run.

The widow started to her feet.

"Sandy!"

A wild hope had come into her heart.

"They're found!" he forced out breath enough to say.

"O Sandy, alive or—or"—

She could not finish the question; the room seemed whirling round her; she grasped at the chair for support.

"Alive!" he shouted. "Alive, an' a-goin' to live!"

[162]

He started forward, and caught the woman as she fell. The shock of joy had been too sudden and too great, and for a time nature gave way before it.

But it was indeed true. When the men, working at the face of the tunnel, caught the sound of responsive tappings, they labored with redoubled energy, if such a thing could be, and, after another night of most gigantic effort, they broke through into the prison-house, to find both boys unconscious indeed, but alive, alive.

Medical aid was at hand, and though for a time the spirit of Bennie seemed fain to leave his wasted body, it took a firmer hold at last, and it was known that he would live.

In triumphant procession, they bore the rescued, still unconscious, boys in tender haste to their mother's house; and those who ran before shouted, "Found! found!" and those who followed after cried, "Alive! alive!"

How the women kissed their own children and wept, as they saw the lads borne by! How the men grasped one another's[163] hands, and tried to speak without a tremor in the voice—and failed. And how wild the whole town went over the gallant rescue of the widow's sons!

But Jack Rennie, poor Jack, brave, misguided Jack! They found his body later on, and gave it tender burial. But it was only when the lips of Tom and Bennie were unsealed, with growing strength, that others knew how this man's heroic sacrifice had made it possible for these two boys to live.

37

Under the most watchful and tender care of his mother, Tom soon recovered his usual health. But for Bennie the shock had been more severe. He gained strength very slowly, indeed. He could not free his mind from dreadful memories. Many a winter night he started from his sleep, awakened by dreams of falling mines.

It was not until the warm, south winds of April crept up the valley of Wyoming, that he could leave his easy-chair without a hand to help him; and not until all the sweet roses of June were in blossom that he walked abroad in the sunlight as before.

[164]

But then—oh, then what happened? Only this: that Jack Rennie's gift was put to the use he had bespoken for it; that skilled hands in the great city gave proper treatment to the blind boy's eyes through many weeks, and then—he saw! Only this; but it was life to him,—new, sweet, joyous life.

One day he stepped upon the train, with sight restored, to ride back to his valley home. Wide-eyed he was; exuberant with hope and fancy, seeing all things, talking to those about him, asking many questions.

The full and perfect beauty of late summer rested on the land. The fields were never more luxuriantly green and golden, nor the trees more richly clothed with verdure. The first faint breath of coming autumn had touched the landscape here and there with spots of glowing color, and the red and yellow fruit hung temptingly among the leaves of all the orchard trees.

The waters of the river, up whose winding course the train ran on and on, were sparkling in the sunlight with a beauty[165] that, in this boy's eyes, was little less than magical.

And the hills; how high the hills were! Bennie said he never dreamed the hills could be so high.

"Beautiful!" he said, again and again, as the ever changing landscapes formed and faded in his sight; "beautiful! beautiful!"

Before the train reached Wilkesbarre the summer evening had fallen, and from that city, up the valley of Wyoming, Bennie saw from the car-window only the twinkling of many lights.

Tom was at the station to meet him. Dear, brave Tom, how his heart swelled with pride, as, by some unaccountable instinct, Bennie came to him, and called him by name, and put his arms around his neck.

Many were there to see the once blind boy, and give him welcome home. And as they grasped his hand, and marked his happiness, some laughed for joy, and others,—for the same reason indeed,—others wept.

[166]

Then they started on the long home walk, Tom and Bennie, hand in hand together, as they used to go hand in hand, to find and greet the mother.

She was waiting for them; sitting by the window in her chair, as she had sat that dreadful winter night; but there came now no sudden jar to send a pallor to her face; she heard, instead, the light footsteps of her two boys on the walk, and their voices at the door; and then—why, then, she had Bennie in her arms, and he was saying—strange that they should be the very words that passed his lips that awful hour when death hung over him—he was saying, "O Mommie! how beautiful—how beautiful—it is—to see!"

Made in the USA
Monee, IL
21 January 2023

25846704R00024